5 A STEVIE DIAMOND MYSTERY

What's a daring detective like me doing in the doghouse?

LINDA BAILEY

KIDS CAN PRESS

Kids Can Press acknowledges the financial support of the Ontario Arts Council, the Canada Council for the Arts and the Government of Canada, through the BPIDP, for our publishing activity.

Pulbished in Canada by
Kids Can Press Ltd.
29 Birch Avenue
Toronto, Ontario M4V 1E2

Published in the U.S. by
Kids Can Press Ltd.
2250 Military Road
Tonawanda, NY 14150

www.kidscanpress.com

Edited by Charis Wahl
Interior designed by Tom Dart/First Folio Resource Group, Inc.
Printed and bound in Canada

CM PA 97 0 9 8 7 6 5 4

Canadian Cataloguing in Publication Data
Bailey, Linda, 1948–
What's a daring detective like me doing in the doghouse?

(Stevie Diamond mysteries ; 5)
ISBN 1-55074-398-8

I. Title. II. Series: Bailey, Linda, 1948– .
Stevie Diamond mysteries ; 5.

PS8553.A3644W42 1997 jC813'.54 C97-930878-X
PZ7.B34Wh 1997

Kids Can Press is a Corus™ Entertainment Company

This book is for my sisters — Debby Barney and Wendy Bailey — with love.

Acknowledgments

Thanks to the staff of Yuppy Puppies in Vancouver for showing me the dog-walking ropes. Thanks also to Debbie Hodge for comments and advice, and to Lia, Tess, Loren, Liza and Emily for acting as first readers. And thanks, as always, to Charis Wahl for her excellent editing.

CHAPTER

It was Jesse who got the idea that we could catch the Prankster.

For months – ever since the Prankster first started pulling his pranks – the newspapers had been full of articles about the guy. Jesse cut out every one of them and saved them in a shoebox, which he kept under his bed, along with all his other collections. Marbles. Feathers. Coins. Wasps' nests. Potatoes with interesting shapes. Believe me, you would *not* want to crawl under Jesse's bed.

"You're obsessed," I told Jesse when he showed me the articles. "And anyway, the guy's a bozo."

"Am not obsessed," said Jesse stubbornly. "And why wouldn't I be interested in the Prankster? The guy's a *criminal*, Stevie."

I'm Stevie Diamond. Stevie, short for Stephanie. Jesse's my friend and also my neighbour, and sometimes even my detecting partner. Diamond & Kulniki, that's us. Over the past year or so, we've managed to solve a few mysteries together. Nothing huge – I mean, no dead bodies or anything. Still, we've been on TV a few times. Not bad for a couple of kids.

But lately, things had been a little slow. Well, okay, really slow. Jesse couldn't stand it. He had an itch to do some detecting – an itch as bad as chicken pox. The only way he could "scratch" it was to read those articles about the Prankster.

Like I said, he was obsessed. And one day on the way home from school, he tried to drag *me* into it.

"Hey, Stevie, wow! Look at that!" Crouching, he pointed at a newspaper box.

The headline was in giant capital letters. "PRANKSTER STRIKES AGAIN!"

I squinted. "So what did he do *this* time?"

"Just a second. I'm reading."

Jesse's not exactly a speed reader. While I waited, I had plenty of time to think about some of the pranks the Prankster had already pulled on important visitors to Vancouver.

Like there was this famous opera singer – a chubby guy with a beard who you've probably seen on TV. Just before he had to go onstage, his toupee disappeared. In its place was a note. "Have a hairy nice performance. Sincerely, the Prankster."

That's right. Hairy nice. The Prankster had a baaaaad sense of humour. But guess what? The opera singer wasn't laughing. Poor guy had to walk onstage as bald as a golf ball.

Then there was the big-star basketball player who came to town – one of the Chicago Bulls. He got locked in a broom closet in the last few minutes of a game against our Vancouver Grizzlies. One minute he was heading for the bathroom. The next minute there was a blanket over his head and a bunch of brooms falling on him. A little while later, the electronic scoreboard flashed this message: "Vancouver Grizzlies Make a Clean Sweep of Chicago Bulls. Best wishes from the Prankster."

Like I said, baaaaaaad.

He'd pulled a lot of other pranks too, but you get the picture.

Jesse giggled. "This time he *really* did it, Stevie."

"What? Tell me."

"He stole the prime minister's underwear!"

"You're kidding!"

Jesse explained. It seems that the prime minister of Canada – our prime minister – had arrived in town that morning for a big conference of world leaders. The other leaders hadn't shown up yet, so the prime minister took an afternoon nap in his hotel room.

While he was sleeping, his room was robbed. Well ... sort of. When the prime minister woke up, he discovered that a small leather suitcase had disappeared from his closet. It didn't contain anything very valuable – just some socks, a pair of pyjamas and *all* of the prime minister's underwear. A note was taped to the closet wall. "You snooze, you lose. Signed, the Prankster."

"You snooze, you lose," Jesse repeated. "I love it! Hey, Stevie! Snooze? Lose?" He let out a snort-cackle laugh and slapped the side of the newspaper box. I sighed. The Prankster wasn't the *only* one with a corny sense of humour.

"And just think!" said Jesse. "We've got a whole week off school to catch him."

"Excuse me?"

"It's spring break, Stevie. We've got –" he counted on his fingers "– nine whole days to find the

Prankster and get the prime minister's stuff back. You and me. Diamond and Kulniki!"

OK, I'll admit it. For about ten seconds, I got sucked in. After all, Jesse and I had caught crooks before. I could see us handing the Prankster over to the cops. I could even picture the prime minister shaking my hand in front of dozens of TV cameras. "I am *extremely* grateful," the prime minister was saying, "to Ms. Stephanie Olivia Diamond, who showed great courage in locating my polka-dot boxer shorts and my –"

"Wait a minute!" I did a little jerk backwards. "Underwear, Jesse? We're going to spend our spring break detecting for underwear?"

He shrugged. "Not just any underwear. The *prime minister's* underwear!"

I shook my head. "I don't care if it's the queen's underwear. It's dumb. People will laugh at us."

They would, too. The kids in our class would howl. I could already hear them: "Hey, Stevie, is that why they call you guys *private* eyes? Haw, haw, haw."

"The Prankster doesn't even commit real crimes," I told Jesse. "A toupee? Underwear? How do you expect anybody to take us seriously if we take cases like this?"

Jesse bit his lip. He knew I was right. We didn't always get the respect we deserved as detectives. Even though we'd solved four cases, some people still looked at us and thought "Kids!" So we had to be picky. Crimes with dignity – that's what we needed. Crimes with class. A diamond heist, for instance ...

"Too bad the Prankster didn't steal the prime minister's watch," said Jesse, reading my mind. "A watch would be serious enough, wouldn't it?"

I shrugged. "Face it, Jesse, the guy's a goof."

I was sure Jesse would give up then, but no. He said maybe there was a reward for returning the prime minister's stuff. I said forget it, the prime minister was rich. He could buy all *new* underwear. And Jesse said, yeah, but wouldn't that be kind of embarrassing – standing in line in the underwear department when you're the prime minister? And I said, what, are you nuts? The prime minister has servants for that kind of thing. And then we started laughing, thinking about the poor servant who would end up in the underwear line. Jesse said maybe we should go downtown – cruise the underwear departments looking for him. And then we started imagining the prime minister in all kinds of different underwear, and then we started imagining him in *no* underwear, and … well, that got us a little hysterical.

Anyway, Jesse didn't mention the Prankster again all the way home. But on Saturday he came by my house and tried again to talk me into going after the guy. And who knows? Maybe he would have finally worn me down …

Except that on Sunday, I got a job. A real job, paying real money – for the whole week of spring break. Not a detective job or anything like that. Just an ordinary job, walking dogs. It had nothing to do with the prime minister. It had nothing to do with pranks. And it had absolutely *nothing* to do with underwear!

So here's the weird thing. In the end, it was my job that led Jesse and me – in a very roundabout way – to the prime minister's stolen underwear. It was my job that put us right in the path of the Prankster, and it was my job that got us into more trouble than I *ever* want to be in again.

That's right. My job.

And the dogs, of course. One dog in particular.

It's a long story.

CHAPTER

I GOT THE JOB BECAUSE OF DINNY'S LEG. DINNY'S A friend of my mom, and on Sunday she tripped taking out the garbage. This wasn't the first time something like this had happened – Dinny's a little accident-prone. Anyway, she wrecked some things in her knee called ligaments, which meant that she'd have a hard time walking for a few weeks.

The problem was – walking was Dinny's business. Dinny owns Barking Buddies, a kind of day care for dogs. People bring their dogs in the morning, and she looks after them during the day. Mostly that means walking them.

On Sunday just after lunchtime, Dinny phoned our house in a panic. I almost never get up before noon on Sunday, so I was still eating breakfast when the call came. I could tell from my mom's side of the conversation – "Oh dear!" and "How awful!" and "You poor thing!" – that something was going on, but it wasn't till I heard my name that I really paid attention.

"Stevie's off school this week," said my mom. "Yes, spring break. Listen, Dinny, I'm sure she'd be – oh yes, absolutely – no, no trouble at all – she'd be happy to – yes, I'll tell her."

By the time she hung up the phone, it was settled. I was a Barking Buddies employee – for a week at least, until they got someone else. Dinny told my mom I should show up the next morning at eight and report to her assistant, Gaylene Schultz.

"Gaylene will be walking the dogs, too, of course," said my mom, "but there are too many for her alone to walk. So you'll take a bunch, and Gaylene will take a bunch and – well, it will work out fine, I'm sure."

"Uh, Mom?"

"Yes?"

"The only animal I've ever been around is Radical." I nodded in the direction of our big orange cat snoozing on a chair. Radical wasn't much of a walker, and he'd give up one of his nine lives before he'd let me put a leash on him.

My mom nodded. "Dinny thought of that. She said you should drop into Barking Buddies today and pick up some books on dog behaviour. There's a booklet there, too, that Dinny wrote, called 'Barking Buddies Basics.' You can study up tonight and be all ready for tomorrow morning."

So that's how, just after dinner, I ended up riding my bike over to Barking Buddies. Jesse offered to come along. He'd never heard of a dog day care and wanted to have a look. On the way, we stopped at Dinny's house for the key. Dinny limped to the door on crutches. Her knee was – I'm not kidding – as big as a grapefruit. I didn't *say* that, of course. I also didn't ask how a person could wreck her knee taking out the garbage, even though I was dying to know.

As we biked from Dinny's to Barking Buddies, Jesse started talking about the Prankster again. He could do the "legwork" on the case during the day, he said, and we could have "brainstorming meetings" after I finished work.

"No," I said firmly. No way was I going to let Jesse turn us into underwear detectives. I didn't care if he had *ten* shoeboxes full of newspaper articles.

As I opened the door to the day care, Jesse whistled. "Look at this place," he said. "Dog heaven!"

Well, not exactly. But Dinny did sell some pretty fancy dog stuff. It was all laid out on shelves just inside the door. Dog shampoos. Rubber bones and balls. Woolly dog sweaters and plastic dog raincoats. Dog toothbrushes, nail trimmers, seatbelts and flea sprays – at least six different kinds. All sorts of dog food and treats, too, including rawhide bones and beef jerky. There were even real pigs' ears – all dried up and chewy-looking. Jesse winced when he saw them. Some things are hard to take when you're a vegetarian.

The walls were covered with paintings and photographs of dogs, and there was a cabinet full of shiny china dogs – collies, dachshunds, Great Danes, chihuahuas. Off to one side, a carpeted area held a desk, a couple of chairs and a couch. Down the middle of the room was a fenced walkway.

"What's with the fence?" asked Jesse.

"The dogs go through here," I told him, "on their way to the yard out back. See?" I pointed to a sign with an arrow on it and the words "Pooch Playground."

"Great!" said Jesse. "Let's go see the pooches!"

"No dogs today," I told him. "It's Sunday, remember? Barking Buddies is only open on weekdays."

"So who's barking?"

"Barking?" I listened. Jesse was right. Only it wasn't really barking – more like a high-pitched whine with a few barks thrown in.

"That's strange," I said.

"Maybe it's a ghost dog." Jesse let out a long, eerie howl. "Ow-ow-owoooooo!"

Immediately, the whine came back – higher this time, and louder. Something was definitely out there in the playground.

"Better go look," I said, glad I wasn't alone. Jesse followed me down the long hall, past the storage room, the bathroom and a little lounge kind of room with a big couch. I opened the back door slowly and not very wide – just in case whatever was out there had huge fangs.

Sitting in the middle of the yard was the most pathetic-looking creature I've ever seen. It was a dog all right, but you had to look closely to tell. It came about halfway up to my knees, and its fur was smeared in brown muck. Underneath the muck, its hair was all matted and tangled in bumpy knots. When I looked closer, I could see why. Burrs! Those prickly clingy seeds that grab onto anything that walks by. The dog was covered in them.

When it spotted us, it whined in this sad little voice that sounded more like a cat than a dog. Its tail started thumping on the cement.

"What happened to you, pal?" asked Jesse as he stepped out into the yard.

The dog toddled over, and Jesse reached out to pat him. Then he made a face. "Phew! What's that smell?"

"He must have rolled in something."

"Like what?" Jesse stared at the smears.

I took a couple of steps closer and sniffed. "Don't ask."

Jesse's face was still wrinkled in disgust, but he was down on his knees now, patting the dog, who was staring up with wet black eyes.

"Poor thing," said Jesse. "He looks lonely. How'd he get in here anyway?"

Good question. I looked around the yard. Mostly, it was just a big open area for the dogs to run around in. There was a grassy part, a large paved area and a small fenced-off corner with a sign that said "Jail." That was where dogs got sent when they weren't behaving. The whole yard was surrounded by a high wooden fence. There used to be a door in it, but Dinny decided there were too many big trucks driving down the back lane, and she'd had the door boarded off.

"Do you think it could have jumped the fence?" asked Jesse.

I glanced up. The top of the fence was three heads taller than me. I glanced down at the dog.

"Not a chance."

"Well, maybe it got left here on Friday night by mistake?"

I shook my head again. "Dinny would never do that. Anyway, what about these smears? And the burrs?"

“Maybe you should phone Dinny. Tell her what the dog looks like.”

“Good idea,” I said. “What *does* the dog look like? Underneath all that gunk, I mean.”

We both stared at the dog, who whimpered and blinked back.

“Good question,” said Jesse.

The three of us – dog, me, Jesse – just stood there in the middle of the yard.

“Well, one thing’s for sure,” said Jesse. “We can’t just leave him like this. We’ll have to give him a bath.”

“A bath?” I shuddered. The last time I bathed Radical, it had taken two weeks for my scratches to heal. “Do you know *how* to bath dogs?”

“What’s the big deal? Soap him up and rinse him down, right?”

I really, really, *really* didn’t want to do this. But it was one of those times when you don’t have a choice. The dog *did* need a bath. Badly.

“Okay,” I said finally. “If we’re going to do it, let’s do it. Fast!”

The trouble was, there was no fast way to do it – at least not at Barking Buddies. The only sink was a tiny one in the bathroom that wouldn’t have held a hamster. There was a hose out in the yard, and I guess we could have hosed the dog down, but it was cold out, and he was already shivering. After a while, it became obvious – we needed a tub. That meant we’d have to take the dog home.

“I can’t believe I’m doing this,” I said as I emptied out my backpack. “Here, quick, drop him in. Ugh! Ick! Let’s get *out* of here!”

I had the idea, you see, that as long as the dog was on my back and I kept moving, I could stay ahead of the smell. Mostly it worked, too – except for a few horrible moments as we scrambled around looking for the books I was supposed to pick up. Once we were on our bikes, it got better. I sucked in fresh air and pedalled fast. The dog sat quietly in my pack with just its head peeking out.

Lucky for us, my parents were out at a play. I sent Jesse and the dog-filled backpack into the bathroom, while I made a quick call to Dinny. *Tried* to make a quick call. When I heard the busy signal, I headed upstairs.

Jesse was perched on the edge of the toilet seat with the backpack on his lap and the dog's head poking out the top. Ears cocked, tongue hanging out, the dog stared at the gushing tap in the tub. He looked – and smelled – as bad as ever.

"We're going to need all the help we can get," I said. Opening the cupboard, I handed Jesse a quarter-full bottle of Peaches & Cream bubble bath. "Let's start with this."

He emptied it into the tub.

"Throw this in, too." Handing Jesse the Autumn Passion bath salts, I stared sternly at the mutt. "I hope you appreciate this, dog. It was part of my dad's Christmas present to my mom."

"He appreciates it," said Jesse quickly, as he dropped the bath salts in. "Don't you, dog?"

The dog barked happily.

"Water's ready," said Jesse, testing it. "Put him in."

He didn't appreciate it.

The second the dog's feet touched the water, he

started acting as if we were trying to drown him – splashing, squirming, scrabbling up the sides of the tub, barking so loudly I was sure the neighbours would complain. Even though the dog wasn't much bigger than a large rat, it was really hard to hold on to him. Jesse was dumping on shampoo, but only about half was actually hitting the dog.

"Hold still, dog," I grunted. "Here, let's – Jesse, can you rub it in over his – hold *still,* dog!"

"Is it coming off, Stevie?"

"I think it – oof – try to get his – HOLD STILL, DOG!"

Within seconds, the water in the tub was an icky grey, and the smell of bubble bath combined with whatever-it-was was enough to make you retch. We soaped, scrubbed and wrestled with the dog. Mostly we wrestled. Finally, after what felt like an hour, we rinsed the dog off and pulled the plug.

"Somebody should give us a medal." Jesse collapsed onto the toilet seat, his white T-shirt soaked and covered in brown smears. The dog was on his hind legs, trying to get out of the tub.

"What do you think?" I asked. "Does he look any better?"

Jesse craned his neck and squinted. A smirk crossed his face. "Uh, Stevie?"

"Yeah?"

"It's … not a he."

I looked. "Oh. Right. Does *she* look any better?"

"A bit. At least the muck is gone. I think she's supposed to be white. But the burrs are still there."

Jesse was right. The dog's long hair was grubby grey now instead of brown, but the shampoo hadn't even touched the tangles.

"What now?" asked Jesse.

I thought for a minute. "Conditioner."

"What?"

"That's what I use on my hair when it gets tangled. It kind of loosens things up."

Jesse couldn't argue. Between the two of us, I am definitely the expert on hair. I have at least ten times as much as he does, and mine is what commercials call "hard to manage." This means that combs get stuck in it. Sometimes they even get *lost* in it.

We tried both kinds of conditioner in the cupboard, the one with ultra-shine and the one with vitamin E. We also tried a frizz-tamer and some stuff that's supposed to fix split ends.

The dog stayed knotty.

"Hopeless," said Jesse.

"Nah, there's got to be – hey, wait, here's something!" I handed Jesse a package I'd discovered behind a twelve-roll pack of toilet paper.

Jesse peered at the package. "Henna. Isn't that a dye?"

"Some kinds are. But this kind just makes your hair smooth and shiny. My mom's used it on my hair a couple of times."

Jesse eyeballed the dog and shrugged. "She couldn't look any worse, right?"

CHAPTER 3

HALF AN HOUR LATER, WE RINSED THE HENNA mixture off.

"I thought you said it wasn't a dye." Jesse's voice was hushed.

"It's not." I shut my eyes tight and then opened them again quickly.

"So why is the dog green?"

Green? Well, not exactly.

I mean, she wasn't green like a forest, or green like a Granny Smith apple. She wasn't sea green or emerald green or lime green either. More than anything else in the world, she looked like the kind of horrible, grungy creature that crawls out of the swamp in a midnight movie. I'm talking the colour of scum. They don't even *have* that colour in crayon boxes.

"Stevie?" Jesse's voice was *really* quiet now. Almost a whisper.

"Yeah?"

"Check out the burrs."

I looked. Then I touched.

Perfect. The dog was now burry *and* green.

"What happened?" asked Jesse.

I picked up the henna package. In the place where it usually said "natural," it said "black." This was my first clue. My mom's hair was starting to go grey. She'd been talking a lot lately about "evening the colour out."

"Uh-oh. I think my mom was going to dye her hair with this."

"Your mom was planning to dye her hair green?"

"Of course not!" Lifting the dog out of the tub, I set her on the bath mat. "It was black dye."

If I'd known more about dogs, I might have been able to predict what happened next – or even stop it. As it was, I only had time to yell "Watch out!" before the dog did a wild shake, spraying water across every surface in the room – walls, floors, mirrors, clothes, skin.

Jesse moved first. Snatching up a purple towel, he did a terrific drop-dive, throwing the towel over the dog like a net and scooping her up so that only her little green head stuck out.

I glanced at the spattered walls. "My parents are going to *love* this."

"Never mind that." Jesse squirmed as the dog nuzzled his neck. "How come she's green?"

I picked up the henna package. It was soggy, but the tiny-print directions inside were still dry.

"Aha! Listen to this: 'If you are using this product on *blonde* hair, be sure to use Henna Prep first to avoid a greenish tinge.'"

"Tinge?" Jesse stared at the face peeking out of the towel. "You call that a *tinge?"*

I winced. "I guess doggy here used to be a blonde."

Jesse shook his head sadly. "Don't you pay *any* attention in Study Skills class, Stevie? Ms. Rizzolo has told us a thousand times, read *all* the directions – carefully, from beginning to end – before you start."

"Geez, Jesse, it wasn't a math exam."

He sighed. "Isn't there a way to – you know – undye it?"

"It says here that the colour will wash out." I read further. "But not until after fifteen to twenty shampoos."

"How often do dogs shampoo?"

I shrugged. "If they're like cats, not very often."

I slumped to the floor. Suddenly, I felt totally crummy. A little lost dog gets into my clutches, and what do I do? I dye her scum green. This was *not* a great start to my career as a dog professional.

The dog wriggled out of the towel, trotted over and licked my face.

"At least she doesn't hate us," said Jesse.

"Wait till she looks in a mirror."

Jesse patted the dog gently, trying to avoid the knots. "There must be a way to get these burrs out."

I shook my head. "It reminds me of when I was six and got bubble gum in my hair. Nothing worked."

Jesse grinned. "So what happened? You just gave up and became a gum head?"

"Not exactly. We – Jesse! That's it!"

"That's what?"

"Wait here."

In no time, I was back with two pairs of scissors – a big silver pair that my mom used for sewing and a smaller pair of old school scissors, the kind that have blunt ends so you don't stab yourself.

Jesse's eyes widened.

"Relax," I told him. "We're just going to give her a little haircut. That's what my mom did when the gum got stuck."

"Gee, are you sure? I mean –"

"We've got nothing to lose," I said, handing him the sewing scissors. "She couldn't *possibly* look any worse."

❖ ❖ ❖

Wrong again.

"Oh man," moaned Jesse. "And I thought she was ugly before."

The dog looked like she'd gotten caught in a fan. There were long bits of hair and short bits and a few almost bald bits – all of it that same horrible brownish green.

Problem was, the dog wouldn't sit still for a haircut any more than for a bath. We had to cut the burrs off while she squirmed and wriggled and tried to jump on us. It wasn't *our* fault that the haircut didn't turn out exactly even.

"But ... don't you think she looks ... happier now?" I asked. The dog was leaping around and wagging her tail as if she'd just shucked off a heavy coat.

I remembered what my dad had said after my bubble-gum haircut. "It's only hair. It'll grow."

I said it now to Jesse.

"I guess so." He didn't sound convinced. "Here, dog, you poor thing! Hey, Stevie, what'll we call her?"

I shrugged. “We don’t have to call her anything. We’re just looking after her till we find her owner.”

Owner. It was a word we hadn’t said before. I hadn’t even *thought* it before.

“Maybe we won’t find the owner right away,” said Jesse. “It could take days, right?”

“Weeks,” I said, wondering how long it takes dog hair to grow.

“Yeah, weeks!” Jesse’s voice was almost cheerful. “Or maybe she’s a stray. Yeah, I bet she’s a stray. We have to call her *something,* Stevie.”

“What’s wrong with Dog?”

He gave me a disgusted look. “How would *you* like it if people called you Girl?”

I saw his point. “Got any ideas?”

His forehead wrinkled. “How about Lassie?”

I gave him a look.

“Okay, forget Lassie. What about Rover? Or Spot?” Then, seeing my face, he mumbled, “I guess I’m not very good at this.”

“We need something interesting,” I said. “Something that really suits her.”

We both stared at the dog, who was lying on the bath mat, her chin on her paws. All I could think about was those midnight movies. The dog was *exactly* the colour of that murky, gloomy ooze the creature crawls out of.

The name just popped right out of my mouth. “Swampwater.”

There was a pause. Then Jesse grinned. “Swampwater. Perfect!”

❖ ❖ ❖

Somehow I had forgotten all about Radical. When we'd carried Swampwater in, he was dozing on the living room couch and had barely glanced up. And why should he? The dog was just a bulge in a backpack. Nothing for a cat to get worked up about.

After the bath, it was a different story.

"MMMMRRRRRREEOOOOOOW!!!"

In a flash, Radical was up on the china cabinet, his fur standing out so far he looked three times his normal size. His eyes were bulging like grapes.

I couldn't blame him. Bad enough that a dog was trotting around his personal territory as if she owned the place. Add in the fact that the dog was grunge green and practically bald in spots and, well ... you can see Radical's problem.

"SSSSSSSSST! HRRRRRRRRKKKKK!"

"Radical!" I said. "Settle down. And you – Swampwater! Get back here."

Swampwater had scurried over to the china cabinet and was staring up at the cat. Her ears were flat, and her little white teeth were bared in a nasty grin.

"Rrrrrrrrr ..." she growled.

The cat was frozen in a crouch, directly above the dog – fur bristling, eyes popping, claws curled tight. If I were the dog, I would have been terrified.

I tapped Jesse on the arm. "Maybe you should take Swampwater home now."

"Home? Home where?"

"Where do you think? To your place."

"*My* place! What are you talking about? My mom's allergic."

A new animal noise came rumbling from the top of the china cabinet. It sounded like a food processor at slow speed.

"Are you telling me," I said to Jesse, "that you expect Swampwater to stay *here?"*

"Well, uh … yeah. I mean, you already have a pet. So one more … well, what the heck?"

On top of the cabinet, Radical was getting into a position I recognized – the one she got into just before she leaped at a bird in the garden. I had about half a second. In one swift move, I lunged and snatched up the little green dog.

"Ssssst!" hissed Radical.

"Hrrrrr!" growled Swampwater.

"The kitchen!" I yelled, leaping backwards. "Radical – stay!"

Jesse and I dashed into the kitchen with the dog. Slamming the door behind us, I glared at Jesse.

He pointed at the door and shrugged. "No problem, Stevie. All you have to do is keep them in separate rooms."

"Me? What about you? Why can't you take Swampwater to your place? Keep her and your mother in separate rooms."

Jesse had the nerve to giggle. "Wouldn't work. My mom can get an allergic reaction right through a door."

"Fine," I said. "We'll just have to take her to one of those places where they look after strays. A dog shelter."

Jesse sucked in his breath. "Are you serious? Do you know what they *do* to dogs in those places?"

"Adopt them out?"

"Oh sure. The cute ones. But what about the ugly ones? The ones nobody wants? The ones that have been *dyed green?* What do you think happens to them?" Slowly, Jesse drew a finger across his neck.

Footsteps thumped outside the house. Bounding off my lap, Swampwater raced to the door and started growling. The door opened and my mom stepped inside.

She took one look and stepped back out.

"Miiiiike!" she screeched. The door whammed shut.

A second later, it opened again, and my dad's head popped in. He stared at the dog. "What –"

"Dad?" I said.

He glanced up, confused. "Stevie?"

"I can explain, Dad. It's a – a Barking Buddies dog."

My dad gazed at Swampwater for a couple of seconds without speaking. Then he said, "Valerie, it's … okay. Stevie says it's a dog. From Barking Buddies."

My mom peered in, too. Both their faces had exactly the same expression – eyebrows up, eyes wide, mouth open. Like a matched pair of salt and pepper shakers.

"That's a dog?" said my mom. "What *kind* of dog?"

"A, um, very rare dog," I told her. Well, that was probably true enough.

My mom turned to my dad. "Have you ever seen a dog that colour?"

He shook his head. "Never."

"They're not very common," I said.

"Rare," added Jesse, nodding.

"And you brought it home from Barking Buddies?" said my dad.

I nodded.

He turned to my mom. "I thought the dogs went home at night."

"They do," I said quickly, "except for this one. Her owner is ... isn't around right now."

So far, so good. I wiggled my eyebrows to let Jesse know he should say as little as possible. If my parents knew the truth, they *might* let Swampwater stay. On the other hand, they *might* drive her straight to an animal shelter.

Swampwater seemed to have a good grasp on the problem. She trotted up to my mom and stood on her hind legs, her little green feet resting against my mom's black pants and her eyes silently pleading.

"Aw, Mike, look. What a cutie."

My dad wasn't convinced. "You're planning on keeping her *here* at night, Stevie?"

I nodded. "She was, um, lonely at Barking Buddies."

My mom was down in a crouch now, patting Swampwater, who was licking her hand and making happy, gurgling noises. "Aw, Mike, it's only for this week. And she'll be gone all day at Barking Buddies, right, Stevie?"

I gulped. "Right."

"What's her name?" asked my mom.

"Er ... Swampwater."

"Swampwater?" My mom's eyebrows wrinkled. "That's a funny name."

"That's a funny *dog,*" muttered my dad.

Giving Swampwater a final pat, my mom stood up straight and stretched both arms above her head. "I'm beat. Think I'll go up and take a nice hot bath."

She was halfway up the stairs before I remembered.

"MOM!!!"

Jesse was right behind me as I tore upstairs. Darting past my mom, we thundered into the bathroom, shut the door and locked it.

"Stevie?" Bangs on the door. "What's going on?"

"It's a bit messy in here, Mom."

Ha! Messy was a spilled drink. Messy was an untucked shirt. This room was messy-multiplied-by-a-billion. Empty plastic bottles, soggy towels in piles, henna splashed all over and – everywhere you looked – clumps of tangled, burry dog hair.

"Jesse and I were ... playing in here, Mom. We'll clean it up."

"Well, make it quick."

"We will. And – Mom?"

"Yes?"

"Could you put Swampwater in my bedroom? She and Radical are ... well, they're still getting used to each other."

Silence. Then, "Stevie? Are you saying that Radical and Swampwater don't get along?"

"Oh sure they do. I mean, they will. Soon. Tomorrow. Just put the dog in my room, okay, Mom?"

Jesse and I worked fast. I took the tub, and he took the rest of the room. Jesse is pickier than me when it comes to cleaning, and he did a way better job. He even found a book that had fallen behind the toilet tank. *Secret Spies and Private Eyes.*

"Hey, Stevie. Can I borrow this?" The pages were curled up from the damp.

"Sure." I glanced around. The room was clean – more or less. My mom would find *something* we'd missed, but that was part of her job. As a mother, I mean.

Ten minutes later, with Jesse gone and my mom safely in the bathtub, I headed into the living room to say goodnight to my dad.

"Swampwater's in your room," he said, looking up from his book. "I gave her some food. I think she was hungry."

"Thanks, Dad. How was the play?"

"Terrific. It's all about an English king, Richard the Third, who – hey, Stevie, that reminds me. Your mom and I saw a lot of streets blocked off downtown, TV equipment all over the place. The president of the United States is in town. The prime ministers of Japan and Australia, too."

Right. I sure hoped these guys could hang on to *their* underwear better than the Canadian prime minister hung on to his.

"They'll probably be on the ten o'clock news," said my dad. "Want to take a look?"

I shook my head. Who had time for presidents and prime ministers? I had more important things on my mind – like the gang of dogs waiting for me at Barking Buddies in the morning. I was starting to worry, just a little. What if the dogs were really big? What if they were mean?

And now there'd be an extra. Swampwater would have to go with me.

"'Night, Dad. I'm off to bed."

Not so easy. There was a guard cat waiting at my bedroom door. Uh-oh. Radical was expecting to sleep where he slept every night – in the bottom bunk of my bed.

"Sorry, Rad," I mumbled, slipping past him into the bedroom. I shut the door firmly behind me.

Swampwater, who'd been nosing around in my closet, came trotting out to give me a sniff. Then she smelled her way around the room, checking out my CD player, my bed, my desk, my stuffed animals and my books. When she got to the permanent pile of dirty laundry in the middle of the floor, she started digging and turned up an old salami sandwich. Cool. I was wondering what had happened to that.

I looked around for something Swampwater could sleep in. Not Radical's bunk. He was already upset enough about being locked out. If I gave his bed away, he'd probably report me to the Society for the Prevention of Cruelty to Animals.

There was only one choice. I dumped my comic book collection out of its cardboard box, turned the box on its side and tucked in a pillow.

"Here, Swampwater. Beddy-bye."

Swampwater stepped slowly towards the box. Crawling inside, she turned around twice, then lay down.

"Good girl," I said. "See you in the morning."

A horrible sound drifted in from the hall.

"Rrreeeeeeeeoooooooow." The cat. Pouting.

"Hey, Radical! Shush!"

"Arreeeeeeeeeeeeoooooow." This time, he added some panicky clawing on the door.

He howled while I put on my pyjamas and kept it up while I got into bed. He was still at it as I tried to read the first page of "Barking Buddies Basics."

"Stevie?" My dad's voice, yelling, from the living room. "What's wrong with Radical?"

"Nothing, Dad."

Muttering a bad word, I jumped down from my bunk. Swampwater was already dozing in the box. Maybe with a bit of luck, I could play switch-the-animals. Picking up the box as if it were a crate of eggs, I carried it to the door and set it down. Then, turning the doorknob, I pulled the door open a crack. Just as I expected, Radical shot inside and raced like a bullet to his bunk. I picked up the box again – gently, gently – and put it out in the hall. Then I stepped back inside my bedroom and shut the door.

Success!

Giving Radical a goodnight pat, I climbed back up to the top bunk and opened "Barking Buddies Basics."

Page 1.

From out in the hall came a new sound. "Awwwwwooooooo."

Ignore it, I told myself.

"Aarrroooooo."

"Hey, Stevie? Is there something wrong with Swampwater?"

"Ow-ow-awoooooooooooooooooo."

"No, Dad," I hollered as I bounded to the floor again. "She's fine! Everybody's fine! We're all fine, fine, fine!"

Before I opened the door, I gave Radical a stern look. "You! Stay where you are!"

I opened the door in mid-howl. "And you!" I said to Swampwater. "Put a sock in it!"

The howl died out as I carried the box, with its load of green dog, back into the room. But as soon as I set it down, the growling-hissing-snarling started up again.

Enough! Didn't these animals know who they were dealing with? Stevie the Grouch, that's who, and she was *not* going to be pushed around by a mangy little dog and a puffed-up old tomcat. Pointing my finger at Radical, I stared him straight in the eye and gave him my best imitation of a parent at a noisy sleepover.

"Go – to – sleep!"

Radical bristled. He let out a throaty growl. Then, burying his nose in his fur, he got it down to a grumbly purr.

Next I pointed a finger at Swampwater. I gave *her* the Evil Eye.

"Not – one – peep!"

Swampwater glared back for a moment. Then, ducking her head, she let out a sulky whimper and dropped onto her pillow.

I stood there for a few minutes, finger pointed, until I was sure they meant it. Then, slowly, I climbed back into my bunk.

"Barking Buddies Basics."

Page 1.

The problem with "Barking Buddies Basics" was that it was a little *too* basic. Hours of operation. Rules for picking up your dog. Cost by the day or the week. I closed it and opened the dog book I had scooped from the bookshelf at Barking Buddies. *Everything You Ever Wanted to Know About Dogs* by Leopold Zimmer. It was a lot more interesting than day-care rules.

Chapter 1 was called "The Wolf Within," and it was all about how dogs are really wolves in disguise.

Well, okay, not actually in disguise, but wolves *are* the ancestors of today's dogs. It seems that thousands of years ago wolves began to hang around human villages, hoping to sneak some garbage. After a while, people started taming the wolf pups. Gradually, over lots of generations, the animals got tamer and friendlier, until finally what you got was dogs.

But here's the thing that made me nervous – this Zimmer guy said that dogs *still* have wolfish habits. Like, they're still pack animals and love to hang around in groups. Barking Buddies was a group. Did this mean that tomorrow, I'd be smack in the middle of a wolf pack?

And there was another thing that worried me – every pack has a leader, called the "alpha" or "top" dog. The other dogs or wolves all know that the alpha is the boss. So if a human being is going to get along with a dog, then the *human* has to be the alpha. The dog has to know you're in charge.

Oh boy. Maybe Zimmer should have called his book *Stuff You Never Really Wanted to Know About Dogs*. How was I going to convince a bunch of strange dogs that I was their leader? Why should they listen to me? I didn't even have a tail.

Wait a minute.

I'd already done it once, right? When I'd put Swampwater to bed, who was top dog then? Me! Stevie Diamond. I'd even done the things that the book said alpha wolves and dogs do – I'd stood above Swampwater, I'd stared directly into her eyes, and I'd used a low warning voice.

I'd been top cat with Radical, too.

Right! I already *knew* this stuff – by instinct. All I had to do tomorrow was remember my simple basic Stevie-Diamond-Top-Dog Technique. Look them in the eye. Use a low warning voice. Stay in charge.

I could do it. Sure I could. Even if they were big. Even if they were mean.

I let out a little growl – just for practice – and turned out the light.

CHAPTER

MY DAD WAS MAKING PORRIDGE WHEN I CAME downstairs the next day.

"Morning, Stevie." Grinning, he held up a huge glop of the stuff on the end of a spoon. "I thought you should have something warm and filling for your first day at Barking Buddies."

"Thanks, Dad."

I put Swampwater down on the kitchen floor and shut the door to keep Radical out. Then I checked the canned cat food, looking for the doggy-est choice. Tuna. Chicken. Lamb. Salmon. Lamb, I decided, emptying half a can into a small plastic bowl.

Swampwater wasn't picky. She gobbled it down.

My dad gave me some porridge. I mixed in a handful of raisins and a sprinkling of chocolate chips, adding a swirl of maple syrup. My dad and I have this deal: I'll eat his porridge, as long as he doesn't say anything about what I put on top.

"Keep your eyes open when you're out today," he said, digging into his own porridge, which was naked and boring except for a puddle of milk. "The city's full of presidents and prime ministers. Maybe you'll spot one."

"That would be neat. What are they doing here anyway?"

He looked pleased to be asked. After glancing at my porridge, he added a handful of raisins to his. Then he reached for the chocolate chips.

"It's called the Pacific Nations Summit, Stevie, and –"

"Why do they call it a summit?" I asked.

I *knew* what a summit was – the top of a mountain. Were all these old guys in suits going to hike up one of the mountains around Vancouver? Have a meeting on top?

"Good question," said my dad. "It's called a summit because it's a meeting of leaders at the highest level. This one is for leaders of countries that border on the Pacific Ocean. They're here to talk about trade mostly. Also defence and immigration. Fishing too. You see, back in 1953 ..."

1953? Better nip this in the bud.

"Thanks, Dad. I get it."

What I was *really* interested in, of course, was the security people. There'd been a lot of stuff in the newspapers about security for the visiting leaders. It sounded like Vancouver would be crawling with police. There'd be the regular city police, of course. Also a lot of Mounties. My dad said the Mounties who hung around the prime minister might even be wearing their fancy red jackets. (Mostly, they wear navy blue these days. Easier to clean, I guess.) I figured there might also be a few undercover police types wandering around, dressed like ordinary Vancouverites.

And then, of course, there were the Secret Service guys – the ones who hang around the president of the United States. I saw them in a movie once, which is how I know what they're called. Secret Service. In my opinion, that's a truly great name – although I don't see how they can be a secret if someone like *me* knows about them. Anyway, these guys should be easy to recognize – sunglasses, suits, walkie-talkies. If you've seen the movie, you'll know what I mean.

Yeah. Mounties and Secret Service guys. I wouldn't mind seeing *them* when I went out dog-walking.

I slurped down my last mouthful of porridge. "Gotta go, Dad. Can you feed Radical? Thanks."

Swampwater sat quietly in my backpack as I pedalled through the damp morning air to Barking Buddies. Rush hour was starting, so I stayed on the quiet streets, away from the heavy traffic.

At exactly 7:59, I walked into Barking Buddies. Gaylene was already there, sitting behind Dinny's desk, scrawling something in a notebook. I'd met Gaylene a few times before when I'd visited Barking Buddies, but I didn't really know her. She was taller than me and thin, in a stringy, muscular way. I remembered my mom saying that she worked out at some gym – and maybe did karate, too. She wore plum-coloured lipstick, which made her skin look really pale, and her short hair was almost blue-black. Bright silver earrings flashed on her ears.

"Oh, Stevie! You're here." She blinked as she checked her watch. "A minute early, too. Good. Dinny said you'd –"

She stopped. Stared. Her mouth dropped open.

I glanced over my shoulder. Uh-oh. Swampwater's head was poking out of my backpack.

"Woof!" she said to Gaylene.

"It's a dog, Gaylene. See?" I shrugged off the pack and put Swampwater on the floor.

Gaylene peered over the desk. "What dog? Whose dog?"

"Oh. Well, mine, I guess. For now, anyway."

"Your dog?" Gaylene's silver earrings danced as she glanced from Swampwater to me and back to Swampwater. "Dinny never said anything about you bringing an extra dog."

"Oh, Swampwater won't be any trouble," I said, hoping I was telling the truth. "I'll look after her myself. You won't even know she's here."

Gaylene's forehead wrinkled, then her nose. "She's awfully … funny-looking."

"You think so?"

Just then, there was a loud bark outside.

"Customers!" Gaylene snapped to attention. "Listen, Stevie, some of our clients have beautiful dogs. Show dogs, see what I mean? Do you think you could take your, um, Dishwater out to the yard while they're arriving?"

"Swampwater," I said. "Sure, Gaylene."

"And, Stevie?"

"Yes?"

"Call me Ms. Schultz. Especially when the customers are here. It shows … um, respect. Okay, dear?"

Dear? Ms. Schultz? Gaylene was probably twenty-two, tops. How come she was acting like a school principal?

But hey, I'd never had a real job before. Maybe

this was how people did things in real jobs.

"Okay, Ms. Schultz."

Sounded like a sneeze.

I was worried that Swampwater might flip out when she saw the Pooch Playground again. Like, maybe it would give her nightmares for life. But no. She toddled out happily and settled down in a corner.

"Stay," I said, hoping she knew what that meant. "I have to go help Gaylene."

Swampwater barked a see-you-later kind of bark, and I dashed back to the front office.

Dinny's customers came in all shapes and sizes, and so did their dogs. The first to arrive was a large black poodle named Lulu. Her owner was a little old guy in a baggy suit. His name was Mr. Lipkus, and he had soft warm hands, as I discovered when he shook one of mine.

"Always a pleasure to meet another dog person," he said with a shy smile.

I smiled back.

Next came a beagle named Walter, owned by a tall guy with thick glasses and a bushy grey beard. Then a cocker spaniel named Sally showed up with a frantic-looking woman carrying a briefcase overflowing with papers and files. Daphne the Dalmatian was led in by a sophisticated woman with long white hair and lots of make-up, wearing a red and black cape. One thing I noticed was that a lot of the owners were on the old side. Older than my parents, I mean. Maybe they needed help to exercise their dogs.

"Hey, Stevie! What are *you* doing here?" It was Austin Alderson, from my school. He and a giant

German shepherd were heading in my direction – fast! If I had to pick which one was alpha, I'd vote for the dog.

"Brutus, stop! Stop, Brutus! Sit!"

Austin looked wrecked. He's my age but a grade ahead. Some kind of a genius, I'd heard. But he didn't look very impressive now. His thick sandy hair was sticking out every which way as if he hadn't combed it, and he was wearing a sweatshirt that said "My Grandparents Went to Tahiti and All I Got Was This Crummy Shirt."

He managed – just barely – to stop Brutus from charging past me to the dog playground. "Sit, Brutus. Sit!"

"Nice dog," I muttered.

Austin rolled his eyes. "We just got him. I *told* my dad he was too big. I wanted a little dog. A spaniel or something. But my dad had German shepherds when he was a kid, so we ended up with –" He pointed.

"Brutus," I said.

He nodded. "Brutus."

"How come you're bringing him here? Can't you exercise him yourself this week?"

He shook his head. "I have math camp."

"Math camp? On spring break?"

Austin smiled. "It's great – I get to do quadratic equations." He glanced at his dog. "My mom and dad are hoping Barking Buddies might settle Brutus down before he starts obedience school next week."

"Obedience school?" I stared. "Isn't he a bit … old for that?"

Austin nodded. "His first owner didn't believe in obedience."

"Oh," I said. "Terrific."

Austin glanced around. "Did you bring a dog here, too?"

I told him about Dinny's grapefruit knee and the job. Brutus, meanwhile, was getting a little bored with our conversation. I could tell by the way he was trying to eat his leash.

"You're going to walk all these dogs?" asked Austin when I was through. "And you're getting paid? Gee, Stevie, you must know a lot about dogs. I guess you –"

He didn't get to finish. Instead, he did a sudden jerk sideways as Brutus bolted towards a fluffy white dog that had just walked in.

"See you later!" yelled Austin.

I shut my eyes and took a deep breath. *What* had I gotten myself into?

CHAPTER

IT TURNED OUT TO BE NOT THAT BAD. ONLY EIGHT DOGS showed up, besides Swampwater. Gaylene said this was normal for a Monday. She said she wouldn't dream of sending me out "untrained," so in the morning we went for what Gaylene called an "orientation session." It turned out to be a two-hour walk.

It started with Gaylene handing me a leather glove with the fingertips cut off. "You'll need this to keep your leash hand from getting blistered," she said as she put one on herself. "This work can be rough on hands."

Then she put the dogs on leashes. I watched carefully so I would know how to do it. She gave me a spare collar and leash for Swampwater, who didn't seem to mind at all. Good. Next Gaylene gathered up the leashes of six dogs – including Brutus – and tied the ends into a giant knot.

"You try it on the three that are left, Stevie," she said. After knotting the leashes on Swampwater, Walter the beagle and Lulu the poodle, I glanced at Gaylene.

"Okay," she said. "Now, hold tight. Whatever you do today, do *not* let go of that knot. Got it?"

I nodded.

"Oh, you'll need these." She held out a bunch of plastic bags.

I stared. "What for?"

"Pet owners have to clean up when their pets make a … a mess on the streets. It's the law."

"What? You're kidding me."

"I certainly am not. There are a lot of dogs in Vancouver. What do you think the streets would be like if pet owners just ignored the messes?"

I decided I'd rather not think about that.

At first, the walk was more like a run. The dogs were really excited to be outside. As soon as we got out the door, a couple of big ones broke into a trot, and the others followed.

"Are they going to run the whole time?" I asked, galloping along behind my three. Swampwater was in the middle, leading the way.

"They'll calm down," said Gaylene, loping along comfortably. "In the meantime, just hold on to those leashes."

We ran to the end of the block, and then we ran another half-block before we slowed to a jog. We finally walked in the third block. The dogs on Gaylene's leashes were all bunched up together, and sometimes they'd switch positions. Gaylene was watching for this, I noticed, and she'd either move the dogs back or reorganize the leashes.

"Watch those leashes, Stevie. You can't always stop them from getting tangled, but you have to straighten them out before it gets too bad."

The dogs seemed to get along pretty well. I asked Gaylene if they ever had fights.

"Most of them are pretty well trained," she said, "and they know one another – except for Dishwater, of course. Also, when they run together like this, they think of themselves as a pack. Remember, dogs are close cousins of wolves."

Some closer than others, I thought, staring at Brutus. He was half a head in front of Gaylene's pack now, tongue hanging out, straining at the leash. Bonbon, the little white fluffball who was running beside him, had edged away as far as he could get. Bonbon kept darting nervous looks sideways, but as far as I could tell, Brutus was ignoring him.

As the blocks went by, I started to feel pretty pleased with myself. Remembering what I'd read in *Everything You Ever Wanted to Know About Dogs*, I felt sure that, in my group at least, I was top dog. Swampwater, Walter and Lulu all sat and stayed whenever I told them to. Gaylene was pretty alpha in her pack, too, if you didn't count Brutus. He seemed to think he was Top Dog of the World and wouldn't do *anything* without an argument.

We moved onto Burrard Street, a bigger street with more people. Most of them looked shocked when they first spotted the dogs – especially the little greenish one. Then they almost always smiled. Gaylene had put little checkered red and white scarves around the dogs' necks, and they did look pretty cute.

Every once in a while, Gaylene would stop to redo her leash knot.

"Sit," she would say to each of the dogs in turn.

"Sit, Daphne. Sit, Bonbon. Sit, Napoleon." If they wouldn't sit, she'd push their backsides down until they did. Some of them sat down and jumped right up again. On one stop, Gaylene had to tell Brutus to sit down four times. Reminded me of a kid I knew in grade one.

"Don't try to retie the knot until every one of them is sitting down," Gaylene told me as she untangled and retied. "When they're all calm like this, you can take your time. Brutus, sit!"

We followed Burrard to the turn-off to the beaches. Fifteen minutes later, we were walking beside the ocean. It was a lot windier by the water, and the dogs seemed to like that, or maybe they were enjoying the squawking of the seagulls and the fishy smell of the water – or maybe even the snow-topped mountains across the bay. Anyway, the dogs broke into a trot again.

I had to use my first plastic bag when Walter made an unscheduled stop on the beach path. Gaylene showed me how to turn the bag inside out to do the scoop, so that I would end up holding the clean outside part of the bag.

"Yeah, but … what do I do with it now?" If somebody had told me that I'd end up running around the city holding a bag of dog doo, I might have thought twice about this job.

"There's a garbage can farther along."

Wonderful.

After walking a long way down the beach, we wandered back towards Barking Buddies through the regular streets. The spring flowers were out – daffodils and tulips – and there was plenty of bird and squirrel action, but the dogs didn't pay much notice. Even a fat grey cat snoozing on a doorstep didn't get their attention. But they did get excited whenever they saw another dog – even from half a block away. First one dog would bark, then another, and another, until finally they were all woofing and hauling on their leashes.

"How come they do that?" I asked. "Go nuts over other dogs?"

Gaylene shrugged. "I guess it's because the other dog isn't part of their pack."

After one untangling of leashes, Brutus ended up on the outside of Gaylene's group, while Swampwater was on the outside of mine. This put them right beside each other.

"Careful, Swampwater," I muttered. "That dog could take your head off in one bite."

But after a block or two, it was obvious that Brutus *liked* Swampwater. He kept sniffing her and licking at her face, like a dog kiss. Swampwater seemed to like him, too. I figured it was like making friends with the school bully – you'd better be *really* careful how you do it.

We were on even busier streets now, and more people stopped to look at the dogs. Swampwater surprised me by barking at one of them – a guy with carrot-coloured hair and wearing a brown leather jacket. He must have gotten too close – or maybe it was his hair, which was *almost* as weird a colour as hers. Anyway, Swampwater let out this awful yipping noise that got Brutus growling just loud enough to make Carrot Hair nervous. The guy backed away quickly.

"Sorry," said Gaylene, shooting an annoyed look at Swampwater. "Some of these dogs are a little new."

"Watch yourself, Swampwater," I murmured as we moved on. "Do you want to get kicked out on your very first day?"

The dogs looked happy to arrive back at Barking Buddies. Ready for a rest, I guess. So was I. But the moment the dogs were in the playground, Gaylene said, "Staff meeting, Stevie."

I blinked. As far as I knew, Gaylene and I were the only "staff," and we'd been "meeting" all morning.

"In my office," said Gaylene, nodding towards the front. She peered at her watch. "At 11:15 sharp."

At 11:14, I walked into the office. Gaylene was sitting, hands folded, behind Dinny's desk. I went to sit in the chair beside the desk, but Gaylene pointed at a couple of chairs farther away.

"The staff sits *there,*" she said. "And the supervisor sits *here.*" She pointed at her chair.

I sat.

"I've called this meeting so the new staff –" she pointed at me "– can become acquainted with the rules." Leaning over, she pulled out a copy of "Barking Buddies Basics."

"Oh, that," I said. "You don't have to bother, Gaylene –"

"Ms. Schultz."

"Right, Ms. Schultz. I read that book. Cover to cover."

Little spots of red stood out on Gaylene's cheeks. "Well, that *may be,* Stevie, but there are some *fine* points you might have missed." She tapped on some paper and pens near the edge of the desk. "If you want to take notes, feel free."

The staff meeting lasted half an hour. Gaylene sent me back to check on the dogs a couple of times. Except for Walter and Napoleon, who were play-wrestling in a corner, they were tired out. A couple were even asleep. None of them looked willing to make enough fuss to get me out of the staff meeting.

At lunchtime I ate my egg sandwich on the couch in the front office and read another chapter of *Everything You Ever Wanted to Know About Dogs*. This one was on dog senses. Some of it I already knew – like the way dogs hear softer sounds than us humans. This explains why they bark before their owners even know there's someone at the door. They can hear higher sounds too, like those dog whistles that sound silent to us.

What I didn't know was that dogs don't see colours very well. This was good for Swampwater, I figured – the other dogs wouldn't know how weird she looked. Then I remembered the carrot-haired guy we'd run into. So maybe it *wasn't* his hair colour that got Swampwater so worked up. More likely, the guy smelled funny. According to Leopold Zimmer, smell is a dog's major sense. Some of them have extremely serious sniffers. Bloodhounds, for instance. They can follow a trail halfway across the country. If I stayed in the detecting business, I would *definitely* have to consider getting a bloodhound.

After lunch, Gaylene and I went for another walk, and this time I got to walk four dogs. I felt pretty proud of myself even though the new dog was only Bonbon the fluffball. Bonbon seemed grateful to be farther from Brutus. Not that Brutus noticed. *He* only cared about being close to Swampwater. It looked like he was getting a serious crush on her. Maybe he liked the smell of shampoo.

When we got back to Barking Buddies, Gaylene gave me some clean-up jobs. I was just finishing when Jesse showed up at 4:50.

"Hi, Stevie. I've got my bike. I thought we could ride home together." He smiled at Gaylene. "Hi!"

"Jesse, this is Gay— Ms. Schultz."

"Pleased to meet you." Gaylene bobbed her head at Jesse, then glanced at her watch. "Quitting time's not till five, Stevie."

"Oh," I said. "Well, what should I do till then?"

"You can …" Gaylene glanced around, "tidy those magazines."

There were six of them. The tidying took fifteen seconds. Jesse wiggled his eyebrows at me and plopped into a chair. I glanced over at Gaylene, who was busy with some files. Shrugging, I messed up the magazines. Then I tidied them. Then I messed them up again. Then I tidied them again. Then I looked at my watch. Four minutes to five.

Finally, at 4:59 and about 45 seconds, Gaylene looked up and said, "You may go now." I dropped Swampwater into my backpack. Jesse and I managed to hold back the giggles until we were outside.

"What's with Ms. Schultz?" he said as we got on our bikes. Turning onto a quiet street, we rode side by side so we could talk.

"Gaylene? Who knows? She seems to really like

having somebody to boss around." I told him about the "Barking Buddies Basics" lecture. Then I described the morning walk.

"How's Swampwater doing?"

"Great. She fits right in. And guess what? You know Austin Alderson from school? He's got a dog in Barking Buddies. The world's biggest German shepherd. His name is Brutus."

"No kidding." Jesse grinned. "I can't picture Austin with that kind of dog."

"Neither can Austin," I told him. "Brutus is hard to handle. Even Gaylene has trouble with him."

We rode along in silence.

"Austin Alderson," said Jesse a minute later. "Isn't he the computer nut? The one who hacked into the principal's files on the library computer?"

"Oh yeah, I forgot about that. He got into some letter addressed to the minister of education. He changed it to the 'sinister of education,' right? Everywhere it said 'students,' he changed it to 'prisoners,' and everywhere it said 'principal,' he changed it to 'warden.'"

Jesse chuckled. "I heard the minister thought it was funny. Austin's parents didn't, though. I saw them coming into the office the next day. They looked mad."

Jesse left Swampwater and me outside my front door. I let the dog out of the backpack, and the two of us followed the food smells into the kitchen.

My dad was making a stir-fry. "Hi, Stevie. How was –"

"Sssssssss!"

Radical! Perched on a kitchen chair, his back curved into an arch, his hair standing straight up.

"Rrrrrrruffff!" Swampwater charged.

"Screeeee!" Quick as a shot, the cat was treed on the microwave. My dad dropped a red pepper on the floor.

Oh, for crying out loud! I thought we were *through* with all that. Did I have to prove I was alpha every single night? Pointing my finger at Radical, I did the low warning voice and gave him the Evil Eye. After he shut up, I did the same thing with Swampwater.

My dad stared. "Hey, Stevie. That's pretty impressive." He picked up the pepper. "You look like a real expert."

Expert? I sighed. "I wish Gaylene thought so."

"Gaylene?"

I grunted. "Yeah, except I'm not even supposed to call her Gaylene."

"What *are* you supposed to call her?"

"Ms. Schultz."

"Gesundheit!"

"It's not a sneeze, Dad. It's her name. She says it shows more respect for me to call her Ms. Schultz."

My dad looked surprised. I call all his and Mom's friends by their first names, and they're a lot older than Gaylene.

"Hmmm," he said, tossing some mushrooms into the pan. "Well, maybe Gaylene is enjoying being the boss for a change."

"You can say that again." I realized how much it had all been bugging me – the staff meeting, the Barking Buddies lectures, the magazine-tidying.

"I *know* she's the boss when Dinny's away," I said. "And I know I have to listen to her. She doesn't have to make such a big deal about it."

"Maybe she's insecure." The pan sizzled as my dad added a glop of sherry.

"What do you mean?"

"Well, I'm guessing, but maybe Gaylene doesn't feel very sure of herself. Maybe she's not sure she can handle the job with Dinny away."

"Oh yeah? Well, she's being awfully bossy for someone who isn't sure she should be boss."

My dad shrugged. "People sometimes act in strange ways when they're not feeling good about themselves."

Now I was curious. "Like what?"

He stared at the ceiling while he thought about it. "Well, sometimes they brag or show off, to get attention."

That rang a bell. Alvin Geary in my class. He stuffs liquorice sticks up his nose to get a laugh.

"Or sometimes," my dad went on, "they insult other people so they can feel better about themselves."

Hah! Evangeline Patterson-Blakely, also in my class. She goes around insulting people in such a sneaky way that half the time you don't even know it's an insult until later. Things like "It must be fun to have freckles, Stevie. They make you look so … perky!"

Perky. Right. It took me a *day* to get mad about that one.

My dad sprinkled the stuff in the pan with soya sauce. "If Gaylene felt sure of herself, she wouldn't think it's so important to be called a 'supervisor.'"

I let out a sigh. "Oh well, whatever. She can be the supervisor. I don't mind calling her Ms. Schultz. Heck, I'll call her anything she wants."

"How about Your Highness?"

I grinned. "How about Your Top Dogginess? Or maybe I'll keep it simple and just call her Alpha!"

My dad's eyebrows jumped. "Good one, Stevie. Who's teaching you all this dog stuff?"

"Leopold Zimmer," I told him. "I think I'll read his book till dinnertime."

"Ten minutes. Your mom's on her way."

Chapter 3 of *Everything You Ever Wanted to Know About Dogs* was called "Breeds," and it was all about about how different kinds of dogs got their start. Mostly it was people who created the different breeds. People mated dogs with certain characteristics, trying to make the characteristics stronger in the pups.

Like the dachshund, for instance. Know why it's shaped like a wiener? It's because people wanted a dog who could chase badgers down their holes. So they kept mating dogs who were long and skinny with short legs. And after awhile, they ended up with ... the wiener dog!

Or sheepdogs. I'm talking about the ones that *look* like sheep – the white, woolly kind. They were bred that way so they'd blend in with the herds they guarded. When a wolf came along, he would *think* he was attacking a helpless herd of sheep. Wouldn't he get a shock when one of the "sheep" sank a set of fangs into his hide!

Feeling something on my foot, I glanced down. Swampwater was using it as a heating pad. Hmmm ... what breed was she? I searched through the book, but no luck – Swampwater's haircut and colour had turned her into a mystery dog. All I could do was figure out a few breeds that she *wasn't*. A giant St. Bernard, for instance. A weensy chihuahua.

Radical, meanwhile, was on top of the bookcase, watching us and sulking. I've known Radical for a long time, so I had a pretty good idea what he was thinking. Things like *Who needs you* and *Go jump in the lake*. Not nice – but better than his Cat of Death routine.

He and Swampwater stayed out of each other's way all evening. No more fights. No threats. Not even any nasty noises. At bedtime, they both settled down with hardly any fuss.

I guess that's why it was a shock when the dog-yipping started. It was 4:33 A.M. on my glow-in-the-dark clock. Seconds after that came the cat-yowling. Horrible! I flipped on the light, expecting to see a furious cat-dog ball rolling across the floor. But Radical was right where I'd left him, on his bunk. Swampwater was by the window, yipping hysterically.

"Hey, you guys!" I yelled over the noise.

My bedroom window looks out on to a courtyard. On the other side, apartment lights were blinking on. My pets were waking up the whole neighbourhood.

"Stevie?" My mom's voice from down the hall.

"It's okay!" I hollered. "Go back to sleep, Mom."

It took maybe ten minutes to settle the animals down again. What was *that* all about? Cat nightmares? Sleepwalking dogs?

"Listen, you guys," I whispered when the lights were out again. "I'm a very patient person. But you have to shape up, understand? You have to stop doing this weird stuff."

I waited. Silence. "Have you got that?" More silence. "And that's an order!"

From somewhere in the room came an *extremely* rude noise.

"Oh," I said.

I waited a moment. Silence.

"Well ... as long as we've got that straight."

I said it in a firm alpha voice.

CHAPTER

THE NEXT DAY WAS CLEAR AND SUNNY, WITH A LIGHT spring breeze in the air – and a flat front tire on my bike. My mom and dad had already left for work, so no chance of a lift to Barking Buddies. After wasting ten minutes looking for my bicycle pump, I ran over to borrow Jesse's.

"You must have run over some glass yesterday." Jesse poked at the floppy black rubber. "It's going to need a patch."

"Rats! I'll have to walk." I checked my watch. "Better get moving."

Jesse bit his lip. "I'd lend you my bike, but I think I might, uh, need it later."

No surprise. I knew Jesse would rather hand over one of his teeth than lend out his new black mountain bike. He'd won it in a contest at the video store, and he didn't even like to ride it in the rain. Mud was bad for the tires, he said.

"That's okay," I told him. "I can still make it as long as I walk fast."

Relieved, he offered to keep me company, and as I hurried along the sidewalk, he half walked, half pedalled beside me. Swampwater scurried in front of us, frisky and cheerful.

"Hey, Stevie, was that Swampwater barking last night?"

"You heard her?"

"People five blocks away heard her. A weird yipping noise, right? What was the problem?"

I shook my head. "Who knows? Some argument with Radical, I guess."

Jesse shrugged. "Why don't you just keep them apart?"

I stopped. Glared. "Keep them apart? They both want to sleep in my *room,* Jesse Kulniki. You think it's easy to teach a cat and a dog to be room-mates?"

Then I let him have it – the whole gruesome story of bedtime in Stevie's room, with the dog and the cat and the box and the bunk and the Evil Eye and the sleepover-parent voice and *Everything You Ever Wanted to Know About Dogs*. When I was done, Jesse said I was making a mountain out of a molehill, and *that,* of course, got me as puffed up and spitting mad as Radical when he first met Swampwater. Anyway, we both got a little excited, and I guess we weren't looking where we were going. The next thing I knew – wham! – I was banging hard into something short and soft and knobby, and it was knocking my legs right out from under me, and – whack! oof! – I did a sloppy, hand-scraping, half somersault right over it and ended up sprawled on my stomach on the sidewalk. For a second, I was half deafened by a hysterical yip-yip-yipping sound. Then it slowly faded away.

What??

"I'm going after Swampwater, Stevie!"

I looked up, dazed, to see the back of Jesse's bicycle as he furiously pedalled away. Ahead of him, disappearing around a corner, was a little green blur.

Right in front of my nose was a pair of shoes – pink and white track shoes. I looked higher – pink and grey jogging suit. A woman's face peered into mine. Long brown hair, gold-framed glasses, blinking eyes, rosy cheeks.

"Are you all right, dear?" asked the woman in a worried voice as I picked myself up. Her left hand was holding on to a large blue baby carriage. "You were walking so quickly – and not looking where you were going. You banged right into little Lawrence's carriage."

"I'm okay." I rubbed my elbow and then tried bending my left knee to see if it still worked.

"Goodness, look at your hand." The woman pointed. "You've broken the skin."

I stared at the pinkish scrape across the side of my hand. It stung, but it wasn't bleeding.

"I'm fine."

"Are you sure? No broken bones?"

I shook my head. "Is your baby okay?"

She jumped a little. "Oh dear! Lawrence!" Swivelling, she poked her head into the baby carriage. "Are you all right, darling? Oh, isn't he wonderful? Didn't even wake up. He's a terrific sleeper, my little Lawrence."

I pulled myself onto my knees and then up onto my feet. I guess I must have staggered a bit because Lawrence's mom put a hand out to steady me.

"Stevie? That's what your friend called you, right? Do you want me to take you home, dear? Or to the hospital?"

Gee, it was just a somersault.

"No thanks." I shook out my legs and arms. "Look. Good as new."

"Are you sure?" She glanced down the street, where Jesse had disappeared, and clicked her tongue nervously. "It doesn't seem right to leave you here. Suppose we wait together until your friend comes back."

I couldn't figure out a way to say no, so the two of us – three if you count Lawrence – stood there awhile. The way Lawrence's mom kept fussing over me, talking about ambulances and broken bones and stuff, you'd think I'd been run over by a transport truck. She fussed over Lawrence too, poking her face into his carriage and cooing at him in a nervous-mother voice. In my opinion, she didn't need to worry. If Lawrence could sleep through my somersault and Swampwater's barking, he was tough enough to take anything.

I checked my watch. I was already six minutes late for work. "Listen," I said. "I really have to go."

"Are you sure?" Lawrence's mom peered down the empty street again.

"Positive." I said it in a very firm voice. "Thanks for your help."

"Take care of that hand," she called after me. "Put some antibiotic on it."

By this time, I was pretty nervous about being late for work. I was also worried about Swampwater. Sure, she could be a pain, but I hated to think of her lost and alone again. I ran the last two blocks to Barking Buddies.

Jesse was out front, perched on his bike. As soon as he saw me, he grinned and held up the leash. Leaping around at the other end was Swampwater.

"Hey! Great work, Jesse." Rushing up, I crouched beside the little dog and got a heavy-duty face-licking.

Jesse nodded. "It was work, all right. I had to chase her three blocks – right through a rose bush and over a couple of high curbs. I think I put some scrapes on the bike."

"Oh. Sorry."

He tried to smile. "It's just a bike, right?"

There was a loud bark behind me. Before I had a chance to turn around, a pair of giant paws came down hard on my shoulders. Really hard! For the second time that morning, I lay sprawled out on the sidewalk. Brutus stood over top of me, licking Swampwater's face.

"Hi, guys." Austin Alderson's voice, coming from somewhere behind the huge mass of German shepherd.

"Austin!" I snapped. "Call off your dog, will you?"

"Right, sure. Brutus, come on. Get off her, Brutus. Off! Sorry, Stevie, he doesn't mean anything. He's just so big."

"I noticed," I said, as Brutus's back feet stepped over my shoulders.

"Hey!" Forehead knotted, Austin was peering at Swampwater. "What kind of dog is *that?"*

Jesse's eyes darted to me. "Just a mutt."

Austin stared harder. "Your mutt?"

Jesse shook his head. "Stevie's mutt."

"Thank you very much, Jesse Kulniki," I mumbled.

"I thought you didn't have a dog, Stevie." Austin bent over to get a closer look. Was this guy nosy or what?

"Did I say that? I don't think I said that." Scrambling up, I dusted off my jeans. "Listen, guys, I would love to stand here chatting, but I have this job, see? So ..."

Stepping around Austin, I grabbed Swampwater's leash out of Jesse's hand and ran inside.

Gaylene was waiting. She gave me a grumpy look and stared at her watch in a very obvious way. I tried to explain, but the story sounded dumb, even to me – flat tires, baby carriage crashes, nervous moms. Finally, I gave up and just said "Sorry" a couple of extra times.

Luckily things got better after that. There were twelve dogs today, and Gaylene and I walked them together. This time I had five dogs – Swampwater, Bonbon, Sally, a Border collie named Shep and a very large floppy-eared puppy named Dagwood. Dagwood was a mix – Gaylene wasn't sure of which breeds, but I would have bet a day's pay that he was part Great Dane. Gaylene warned me about this little problem he had – namely, he didn't know which way was forward. He was just as likely to head backwards or sideways.

Fortunately, I also had Shep, who treated me to a first-hand look at how Border collies operate. I already knew, from Zimmer's book, that their favourite activity is herding sheep. If there are no sheep around, a Border collie will herd whatever's handy – the little kids in the family it lives with, or even other dogs. And sure enough, every time Dagwood headed in the wrong direction, Shep herded him back.

"That's why I put them together," said Gaylene.

"Really? You mean Shep's working for Barking Buddies?"

She nodded.

"Maybe we should invite him to staff meetings."

Well, *I* thought it was funny.

We hiked past the boat marina and Granville Market, then followed the path beside False Creek. Some early rhododendron bushes were in bloom – big pink, white and purple flowers. The sun shone, the dogs behaved, and I didn't even mind the pooper-scooping.

It was easy. Fun. I should have *appreciated* it more.

We got back to Barking Buddies just before noon. At twelve o'clock on the dot, Jesse poked his head through the door.

"Stevie? Is it your lunchtime yet?" The second he opened his mouth, I knew something was wrong. The quiver in his voice was so strong, it practically made a tune.

Gaylene told me to be back in an hour, and I hurried outside. Jesse was hunched against the building, his hands shoved deep in his pockets.

"What's up, Jesse?"

He glanced around the busy street nervously. "Not here. Somewhere we can be alone."

"Why?"

He grabbed me by the arm and marched me down the street. When we got to the park at the end of the block, he glanced around again in that super-spy way before motioning me over to an empty wooden bench. Then he checked behind a garbage can to make sure no one was there.

"Jesse, what's going on?"

He sagged as if all the air had been let out of him and pulled a folded newspaper out of his back pocket. "Look! It's yesterday's."

I read the headline out loud. "'Flood Threatens Italian Village.'"

"Not that!" He jabbed at another article with his finger. "This!"

Down in the lower left-hand corner.

"President's Dog Stolen." I sucked in my breath.

"Go ahead, read it." Jesse was cracking the knuckles of his left hand, one after another. "Oh, Stevie. We're in trouble. We're in biiiiiiiig trouble. We're in baaaaaaad –"

"Shh. Let me read."

A dog belonging to the visiting president of the United States was stolen Sunday morning in Stanley Park.

At a press conference today, police spokesperson Karen Thompson stated that the theft occurred at approximately 10:00 A.M. as the dog was being walked in the park by the president's secretary. The secretary had stopped briefly at a water fountain when a cyclist wearing a mask and a white helmet raced past and snatched the dog's leash out of her hand. The secretary attempted to follow the thief, but was unsuccessful.

Police investigating the theft found the following message written in chalk on a nearby sidewalk:

"The Dog is Gone. What a Dog-Gone Shame! Signed, the Prankster."

"Iiiiy! Jesse! It's the Prankster!"

"I know," he said miserably. He was working on the knuckles of his right hand now. For such a big Prankster fan he didn't look the slightest bit pleased. "Stevie, this is awful. This is –"

"Wait! I'm still reading."

> Police believe the crime is linked to a series of other pranklike crimes that have occurred in Vancouver in recent months. The person claiming credit for these crimes is known only as the Prankster.
>
> Police are asking the public to be on the lookout for a flop-eared Skye terrier with a long cream-coloured coat. The dog answers to the name of Marietta.
>
> Police are also asking the public's help in capturing the Prankster. "This time, he's gone too far," said Constable Thompson. "The Prankster may think this is a joke, but it's not. The president is an extremely important visitor, the dog is valuable, and this is theft. We are taking it *very* seriously."
>
> When asked what kind of person the Prankster might be, Thompson replied, "Someone with a clever mind and a juvenile sense of humour. Someone seeking attention." Witnesses described the Prankster as being of medium height and "athletic." He (or she) was riding a black trail bike.

Okay, I didn't want to jump to any conclusions, but I felt sick.

"There's a picture on page six, Stevie."

"It's probably just a coincidence," I muttered as I turned the pages. "It's probably just –"

The dog in the picture was small and whitish and had so much long hair you could hardly see its face – one of those dogs that looks like a mop without the handle. It was sitting on the president's lap. You could tell by the expression on the president's face that he *liked* that dog. A lot!

Jesse's voice had gotten tight and high-pitched. "Marietta," he squeaked, pointing at the caption under the picture. "She was named after the president's great-grandmother."

Neither of us spoke for at least a minute.

Then Jesse asked the Big Question.

"Is it Swampwater?"

I squinted at the photo. It was fuzzy, the way newspaper pictures are. "I don't know. Hard to tell."

"It's her, Stevie."

I shook my head. "Swampwater doesn't look anything like that dog."

Jesse made a weird gurgling noise, like somebody had just poked him in the stomach. "What if somebody cut off most of *your* hair and dyed *you* green? Do you think *you'd* look like yourself?"

I nodded. "It could be her."

"It's her."

"I know how we can find out," I said, not totally sure I wanted to.

"How?"

"We can call her. Using that name – Marietta. See if she comes."

Jesse chewed on his lower lip for a while. "Okay," he said finally, still in that funny voice, "but we should try calling her some other names first. Maybe she answers to anything."

I nodded. "Now. Before we lose our nerve."

We were back at Barking Buddies in less than a minute. I dashed inside. Gaylene was dozing on the couch in the lounge and didn't even open her eyes as I snatched up Swampwater and hurried outside.

"Stand in front of that doorway," I told Jesse, pointing at the car-parts business next door. He backed off till he got to the right place. Carefully, I set the little dog down on the sidewalk.

"Call her," I said.

"Rover?" called Jesse in a quivery voice. Then louder, "C'mere, Rover."

Ignoring him, Swampwater headed over to the grass boulevard. She sniffed around till she found a bare spot and started digging.

"Spot?" called Jesse. "Here, Spot! There's a pal."

More digging.

Not a single doggy glance for Lassie either. Or Fido. Or Bowser. The way Swampwater was digging, you'd think there was a brontosaurus bone buried under that boulevard.

Finally, after a pause that seemed to go on forever – I could tell Jesse was building up his courage, the way you do before you leap into a cold swimming pool – he blurted it out.

"Marietta?"

The dog turned. Her ears perked up. She wagged her tail.

In a voice so quiet I could hardly hear it, Jesse called, "Come here, Marietta. Here, girl."

Swampwater let out two sharp, happy barks. Then she ran to Jesse as straight as an arrow to a bull's eye, leaping against his legs in a frenzy of joy. Jesse was too stunned to even pat her.

Neither of us could speak.

In the end, it was Jesse who broke the silence. It came out as a wail. "Stevie, what are we going to doooooo? We've wrecked the president's dog!"

CHAPTER 7

PANIC! THAT'S WHAT WE WERE GOING TO DO.

The way I knew this was – Jesse had already started. He was making little whimpering noises and rocking back and forth on his heels. Both hands were clenched into fists, and the left one was smacking steadily against his thigh.

"Ooooh, Stevie, we're in trouble. We're in huuuuuge trouble. We're in baaaaaad trouble. We're –"

"Jesse! Get a grip!"

Most of the time, Jesse's a pretty sensible guy. But in a crisis? Not great. Swampwater had backed away from him and was barking nervously. I didn't blame her, but I could only deal with one of them at a time. I snatched up the dog, raced inside and returned her to the playground. When I came out again, Jesse was still standing there, rocking and smacking.

I grabbed his arm. "Let's walk."

"Good idea!" Jesse's eyes darted around wildly as he stumbled into step beside me. "We'll walk – yes! – to Mexico. That should be far enough. Of course, we can't walk all the way, but – hey, maybe we could hitch a ride with a big truck or something – yeah, a big truck, carrying lumber – and we could eat nuts and berries that we pick along the way and –"

"Jesse! You're hysterical. Breathe."

He took a deep breath.

"It'll be okay, Jesse," I steered him to an intersection. "We'll just give her back."

"Give her back? How can we give her back? Didn't you see that picture in the paper? She *used* to be cute, Stevie."

"Will you please calm down? I *know* we can't give her back looking like a swamp monster. We have to clean her up first."

"Clean her up? How?"

"Henna comes out, remember? Fifteen or twenty shampoos?" The light changed, and we started across the street.

"That could take months. You said so yourself."

"Not if we gave her, say, two or three shampoos a day."

He stopped – right in the middle of the intersection – and stared at me. "Are you nuts? She hates baths! You want to spend your whole spring break in the bathtub wrestling with a dog?"

I glared back. "You think walking to Mexico is a *better* idea? Nuts and berries, Jesse? Are we going to sleep in haystacks, too? Drink out of mountain streams?"

BLAAATTTT! A horn blared as a blue truck slammed to a stop just a car-length away. A guy in a baseball cap stuck his head out the window.

"You kids looking to get killed? I got a green light here. Move!"

We moved. In the time it took us to scurry across

the street, Jesse seized onto my bath idea like someone in quicksand grabbing onto a rope.

"You're right, Stevie! That's exactly what we have to do – wash the green stuff out. And if we comb her hair really well and, you know, fluff her up a little, she'll look fine. Well, okay, not *fine,* but ... well, better, right?"

"Right."

We passed a convenience store and a travel agency without speaking.

"Stevie?" Jesse's voice sounded nervous again.

"Yeah?"

"It's not going to work."

"Why not?"

"Didn't you read the part about the black mountain bike? And the white helmet? And the medium height?"

"Yeah." I wasn't sure what he was getting at.

"It's *me!"* He almost yelled it. "Don't you see? They're describing me!"

I stared. Then – I couldn't help it – I laughed. "Come on, Jesse. Do you think you're the only person in Vancouver who owns a black mountain bike and a white helmet? There must be hundreds of people who fit that description."

"What about the athletic part? And the clever mind?"

"Don't forget the juvenile sense of humour," I reminded him.

"What's juvenile?"

"Childish."

"Well, heck! I'm a kid, right? Of *course,* I have a childish sense of humour. Stevie, it's me they're talking about. This whole article is saying just one thing – Jesse Algernon Kulniki!"

"Algernon?"

He winced. "My mom. She read it in a book the week before I was born. I'm just lucky it isn't my *first* name. But never mind that. What am I going to do? They'll come after me, Stevie. They're going to think I'm the Prankster."

"Will you please relax?" I pulled him past the open doorway of a flower shop. "Lots of people have bikes like yours. Lots of people are athletic and have clever minds."

"Yeah," said Jesse, "but how many of them have the president's dog?"

That stopped me.

Excellent point. We *did* have the dog. And if we got caught with her, the police were bound to notice Jesse's black trail bike. Also his white helmet. Also his juvenile sense of humour.

"You're right," I said. "You're in trouble. I mean – we're in trouble."

"Oh geez, oh geez, oh geez, oh geez." Arms stiff, fists clenched, Jesse started bobbing back and forth from one foot to the other. "I wish I'd never seen that dog. I wish I'd never seen you, Stevie. I wish I'd never been born. I wish –"

This is where a movie detective would smack the person hard across the face. For his own good. To calm him down. Because he's hysterical. It always works, too – in the movies – and I can't say I wasn't tempted. But I guess I'm just not the smacking kind of detective. Besides, Jesse might just smack me back. So instead I grabbed him – hard – by both shoulders and gave him an intense alpha stare.

"There's something you're forgetting. We're detectives."

He frowned. "So?"

"So this is a crime, right? We'll solve it."

"You mean ... we catch the Prankster?"

I nodded. "If we can hand over the dog *and* the Prankster, we're off the hook."

With a loud groan, Jesse threw both hands in the air. "That's what I wanted to do in the *first* place, Stevie. *Why* won't you ever listen to me?"

"It's different now."

"Yeah, sure. I'm about to get arrested now. That's what's different."

I opened my mouth to argue, then closed it again. Jesse was right. Somewhere out there, right now, the police were searching. They had asked the public to help, too. Soon the whole city would be looking for this dog. It was only a matter of time before somebody saw through Swampwater's disguise. And then what?

Who would believe that we *found* the dog? What would the police think when they saw the bike and the helmet and – hey! – Jesse's shoebox? It would look like he was collecting clippings about *himself!*

Through four cases – our whole career as detectives – Jesse and I had worked hard to figure out "who done it." Just like in detective books and movies. Now, for the first time, we were on the *other* side. The criminal side. If Jesse and I didn't find the Prankster, chances were excellent that the bad guys "who done it" would look a lot like ...

Us!

CHAPTER

"THE FIRST THING WE HAVE TO DO," I SAID, "IS CALM down." No way were we going to figure anything out if we were flapping around like a couple of terrified chickens.

"Calm." Jesse gnawed hard on his right thumb. "Calm is good."

"Right! Let's go through the whole thing. It started on Sunday morning at ten o'clock, when this secretary person took Swampwater for a walk in the park."

Jesse nodded. "The Prankster swooped down on his bike, grabbed Swampwater and took off. Then what?"

"Exactly!" I said. "Then what? The next thing *we* know is that Swampwater shows up at Barking Buddies, in a locked yard – filthy dirty – by five o'clock in the afternoon. So what happened in between?"

That question led to the question that had been bugging me all along. "How did Swampwater get into Barking Buddies?"

Unless …

Jesse's eyes widened, but I said it first. "Maybe the Prankster *put* her there!"

Nodding eagerly, Jesse skipped along sideways beside me. "Yeah, Stevie! The Prankster left Swampwater in the yard to … to hide her or something. After all, it *is* a dog yard. Maybe he planned to come back and get her later."

Was it possible? Sure. But it opened up a whole bunch of new questions.

"Say we're right, Jesse. Say the Prankster *did* put Swampwater in the Barking Buddies yard. How did he do it? There's no way in – except through the front door of the building."

Jesse's eyes got even bigger. We stopped at another intersection. "Maybe that's it, Stevie. Maybe the Prankster walked in through the front door, just like you and me. Maybe he – or she – has a key."

A key! But that would mean –

"As far as I know," I said slowly, "there are only two people who have keys. Dinny and Gaylene. Are you saying that … one of them is the Prankster?"

Jesse's shoulders rose and fell in a shrug. The light changed, and we crossed.

"Not Dinny," I said, remembering her grapefruit knee. "She had a wrecked leg. No way she could get on a bike."

"Okay," said Jesse, "well, that leaves –"

"Gaylene!"

My mind filled with a picture as bright and clear as TV – Gaylene, in a mask and bike helmet! She was riding a huge black bike, peddling at attack speed as she swooped down on a shaggy little dog in Stanley Park.

My next thought made me pull Jesse over to a bench and sit him down. I snatched the newspaper out of his hand and pointed. "Check this out, Jesse. Gaylene fits the psychological profile of the Prankster perfectly."

Jesse looked confused. "The psycho – what?"

"The criminal's personality – what the police know about what kind of person he is."

"*She* is."

"Right. She. Anyway, the psychological profile of the Prankster is right here in this article. It says the Prankster is seeking attention."

"So?"

"So you know how Gaylene's been acting so bossy? My dad says it's because she doesn't feel good about herself. He says that people who don't feel good about themselves sometimes do funny things *to get attention.*"

"Like steal things?" said Jesse. "Or pull pranks?"

I nodded. "Don't you see? Gaylene fits the profile."

Jesse moved my hand so he could read the article. "Does Gaylene have a juvenile sense of humour? That's part of the profile, too."

I shrugged. "As far as I can tell, Gaylene has no sense of humour at all. But she sure fits the *rest* of the description." I tapped the paper. "See? Athletic. Gaylene's job is walking. And she works out in a gym. What could be more athletic?"

"I don't know, Stevie." Jesse took the paper and folded it neatly. "I always thought …"

"Thought what?"

"Well, you know. I always pictured the Prankster as a … well, a guy."

"A guy? How come?"

"Think about it," said Jesse as we started walking again. "Do you really think some *girl* could trap a Chicago Bull in a broom closet?"

I sighed. Sometimes I think I'm *never* going to get the cobwebs out of Jesse's brain.

"Haven't you ever heard of women astronauts?" I asked him.

"Well … yeah."

"Women police officers? Women basketball players?"

"Well … sure."

"Gaylene takes karate, Jesse."

"Karate?" He grinned. "No kidding! Karate?"

Noticing a crushed pop can on the sidewalk, he gave it a kick. "Well, okay. I guess it's *possible* that Gaylene's the Prankster. But there's something I don't understand."

"What's that?"

He kicked the can again. "Well, if you're right, you and I have just stumbled into the middle of Gaylene's biggest, baddest prank ever. Not only that – we've grabbed the prize! So how come she's not trying to get the dog *back?*"

"Why should she?" I asked. "Swampwater is right under her nose at Barking Buddies every day. We're doing her a favour, Jesse. We're looking after her stolen loot."

He slapped his thigh. "You're right! And if anyone gets wise, *we're* the ones who are in trouble. Oh man, she's smart all right. She's clever. It said so in the profile, and it's true." He gave the squashed can another kick, sending it skittering down the sidewalk. "So what do we do now?"

"Question her," I said. "I'll do it this afternoon. Casually, of course, and very carefully. We don't want her to suspect anything."

"Right. Can I help?"

Uh-oh. Jesse's a *terrible* questioner. He gets nervous. He blurts things out.

"Waste of your time," I told him. "Why don't you go ... check out the scene of the crime? The Prankster's note is probably still there, on the sidewalk in Stanley Park."

Jesse nodded. Picking up the squashed can, he dropped it into a recycling bin. "Know what? Now that we have a plan, I feel a lot better. I even feel hungry. Got any lunch?"

Lunch! I'd forgotten all about it. I glanced at my watch. It was twenty to one, and we'd wandered blocks and blocks away from Barking Buddies – and my lunch bag.

We did a quick jog back. Even so, I barely had time to wolf down half a peanut butter and jam sandwich before one o'clock. Jesse took the rest of my lunch and headed for Stanley Park.

I had to face Gaylene. There are a lot of tough jobs in a detective's life, but one of the toughest is "acting normal." Ever tried it? As soon as you start thinking about it, you forget what "normal" is. The worst moment came when Gaylene told a joke. It was really feeble – something about a guy with a parrot on his head. I didn't even get it. But I laughed so hard, I gave myself a coughing fit. Definitely *not* normal. Gaylene knew it. After she whacked me on the back, she gave me a really strange look.

I hid out in the bathroom for a few minutes, thinking about the joke. Nope. Still didn't get it. But the more I thought about it, the more "juvenile" it sounded. Definitely Prankster material.

It wasn't until we were out walking the dogs that I finally got up the nerve to question her. I decided to start with the bike. First, I told her what kind of bike I had. Then, totally offhand, keeping my eyes on the dogs, I asked, "What about you, Gaylene? Have you got a bike?"

"Sure," she said. "I don't ride it much, though. I usually drive my car."

"Hmmmm," I said, casually. Very casually. "What kind of bike?"

"Brutus, stay!" The muscles in Gaylene's forearms worked as she tried to control the German shepherd. "I will be *so* glad when this dog is trained. Stay, Brutus!"

I waited. A minute later, I tried again. "Is it, like, a ten-speed? Or a three-speed?"

"What? Oh, my bike? It's a mountain bike."

"What, um, colour is it?"

Gaylene gave me a puzzled glance. "Navy blue, I guess. Why do you ask?"

"No reason." This, I decided, would be a very good time to stop and untangle my leashes.

Navy blue. Well, it wasn't exactly black, but it was awfully close. Close enough for the witnesses on Sunday morning to make a mistake?

Okay. New angle. Maybe I could quiz her about some of the earlier pranks. "Do you like basketball, Gaylene?"

"Basketball! What made you think of that? Sure. I used to play it in high school."

I knew it was dumb, but I couldn't resist. "What about opera?"

"Stevie, what's going on? Why are you asking all these questions?"

Okay, I *definitely* should have stopped there. It would have been the smart thing to do. My brain knew this. The problem is, my mouth isn't always as smart as my brain. Before I could stop it, I heard my mouth asking, "What do you think about the Prankster?" My brain was yelling NO, NO, NO!

What happened next was a surprise.

Gaylene ignored me. Totally.

Okay, maybe it was because of the truck that rolled by just then. Maybe she really didn't hear the question.

Or maybe ... she just didn't want to answer it? The truck wasn't *that* loud.

Neither of us spoke for the next few minutes. Then Gaylene turned to me with a stern look. "Stevie?"

"Yeah?"

"Tuck in your shirt. And straighten that collar."

I tucked. I straightened. And for the rest of the afternoon, I kept quiet.

So did Gaylene. No more jokes, not even juvenile ones. The only time we talked was when I paid her for the bottle of Pampered Puppy shampoo. It cost almost ten bucks, but I figured that Swampwater was probably used to the best of everything – and if it got her closer to her real colour, it would be worth it. I bought a couple of cans of Doggy Divine dog food too – one with sliced turkey breast and one with chunks of tenderloin in gravy. Also a rawhide bone and a box of deluxe dog biscuits. If Jesse and I ever had to tell the whole awful story to a judge, at least we could say we had treated Swampwater well.

Just after five o'clock, as the owners were starting to arrive, my mom showed up.

"I ran into Jesse, hon. He said your bike is down, so I thought I'd give you a lift. Hi, Gaylene! How's everything going?" My mom wandered over to the desk, stepping around Sally, who was lying in the middle of the dog path. "I hope Stevie's making your life a little easier this week."

Now here was something I didn't need – a conversation between my mom and Gaylene. I had never exactly *said* that Swampwater's owner was on holiday, but somehow my mom had gotten that idea. Sooner or later, she was bound to ask when this mysterious owner was coming back. I hurried to the playground to get Swampwater. When I got back, Gaylene and my mom were talking about Dinny's knee.

"I know just how Dinny feels," my mom was saying. "I broke my wrist skiing a couple of years ago. Dinny was lucky – at least they were quick in Emergency. *I* had to wait around for hours."

I'd heard this story before. It took at least twenty minutes to tell.

"Mom?"

"It was a nightmare. There must have been a traffic accident or something. Doctors and nurses running everywhere, and meanwhile my wrist was all swollen and throbbing ..."

"Mom?"

She turned. "Yes, Stevie?"

"I'm starving. Can we go, please?"

"Oh. Sure, honey. Good to see you, Gaylene."

The broken-wrist story must have reminded my mom of other family visits to the emergency ward. Before we were halfway home, we had gone through my dad's cut finger, my Uncle Dan's appendix and the time I stuck a dried bean up my nose. We were moving on to the time she *thought* I ate a poisonous mushroom when I spotted the kid on the fence.

It was a high fence, taller than me, and made of wire, and it was around a private school a few blocks from my house. Whenever the school is closed, the janitor locks the gates around the school yard. My mom says it's so nobody can get hurt on the playground equipment and sue the school. But it's got this really terrific basketball court, and teenagers – like the guy I was watching – get in by climbing over the fence. So I was watching this guy climb the fence with one hand as he held the basketball in his other hand, and I was wondering why he didn't just *throw* the basketball over first. Then I noticed this girl waiting for him on the other side, so I figured he was probably showing off for her, like he was some hotshot athlete or something and then –

Ping! I got it. In my mind, the school-yard fence suddenly changed into the fence at Barking Buddies. And instead of a kid holding a basketball, I was seeing – the Prankster! In a white helmet and a mask, holding a dog no bigger than a basketball.

Of course!

The Prankster didn't *have* to go through the front door of Barking Buddies. Anyone who was the slightest bit athletic could climb *over* that fence in a flash!

CHAPTER 9

THE MOMENT THE CAR STOPPED, I GRABBED Swampwater and the bag of dog stuff and sprinted towards Jesse's house.

"I thought you were starving," yelled my mom.

"Later!"

Jesse was alone. His mom is the manager of the Incredible Red Burger Barn, a restaurant near where we live, so most days she's working at dinnertime.

Jesse had news, too. He blurted it out before I even got inside. "I saw the Prankster's note in the park, Stevie. It was written in blue chalk on the sidewalk. And you know what? All the letters were really neat. It looked *exactly* like Ms. Rizzolo's writing."

"Really? Ms. Rizzolo. Our teacher."

Jesse nodded. "Hey, Stevie. You don't suppose –"

"Forget it." I handed him the dog so I could peel off my jacket. "Ms. Rizzolo went to Hawaii for spring break. Anyway, she's not the type."

He frowned. "I suppose not. So, did you find anything out?"

"I'll tell you while we bath Swampwater. This

time we mess up *your* tub."

Fortunately, we had to go past the kitchen on our way to the bathroom – a perfect opportunity to hint that I hadn't eaten for five hours and, even then, I'd had only half a sandwich. After a bit of searching, Jesse came up with an almost full box of cereal – Maple Critters. We gulped it down in handfuls, straight from the box, as we headed upstairs.

Jesse's bathroom was way neater than ours. Everything was pale blue or white, and it all matched – the toothbrush holder, the water glass, the soap dish. The towels looked as if they'd been ironed. There was a thick white oval rug on the bathroom floor. After patting it down with her paws, Swampwater settled into the middle of it.

As the tub filled with water, I told Jesse about Gaylene's mountain bike. He agreed that navy blue could easily look like black if you saw it in a hurry. Then I told him what I'd figured out about the Barking Buddies fence.

He let out a whistle. "You're right, Stevie. The fence is high, but not too high to climb over. So are you saying that Gaylene's *not* the Prankster?"

"I don't know. She did get a little tense today when I questioned her. But even if it's not her, it still has to be somebody who knows there's a dog yard back there – and that means *somebody* connected with Barking Buddies."

"Hmmmm." Jesse bit his lip and thought hard. "You mean, like a customer?"

I nodded. "The problem is – most of the customers are old. You think some old geezer could climb that fence?"

"No way." A second later, Jesse's eyes lit up like a couple of lightbulbs. "But a *young* geezer could."

"A young geezer?"

"Austin Alderson!" Jesse almost hissed the name. "Remember that psycho-whatever-it-was profile? The clever mind? Who's got a cleverer mind than Austin 'the Brain' Alderson? Who's more juvenile? And – wow, Stevie – he's even got a record of pulling pranks. Remember that computer message he sent to the minister of education?"

Could it be? Austin?

"It's him!" Jesse nodded his head rapidly. "It's definitely him."

"Wait a minute. What about that prank with the Chicago Bulls?"

Jesse was grinning now. "Yeah, so?"

"Let me get this straight. You think Gaylene couldn't trap a professional basketball player in a closet – but Austin could?" A memory flashed through my brain – Austin being dragged around Barking Buddies by Brutus.

But Jesse just grinned wider. "He's a guy, Stevie."

"Sure he is, but he's not exactly Mr. Universe."

Jesse looked insulted. "He's the same size as me."

Exactly, I thought. I didn't say it, though. Jesse's a little sensitive, so I was not about to use the word "short." Better stay away from "scrawny" too.

"Listen, Jesse, all I'm saying is that it wouldn't be easy for Austin Alderson to stuff a Chicago Bull into a closet."

"He could do it," said Jesse, nodding. "He's wiry. Like me."

I decided to let it go. If I've learned anything from

working with Jesse, it's this: don't hurt his feelings. *Nothing* can mess up an investigation worse than a sulker.

"Got any paper?" I asked. "I'm going to write this stuff down."

Jesse soaped the dog while I made up a suspect list. The bath went a lot better this time. Maybe Swampwater was happy to have her short haircut, or maybe she was just tired out from all the exercise she was getting, but she didn't move around so much. The Pampered Puppy shampoo worked well, too, if you could judge by the foam it made. Swampwater ended up coated in a thick white lather from end to end.

After a while we started to get goofy with the foam. First, Jesse gave Swampwater a bunch of frothy lumps on her back.

"It's the Loch Ness Dogster!" he said. "Quick, Stevie! Take her picture before she sinks back under the surface."

Next I gave her a pointed head.

"The Dog from Another Planet," I said in a deep, hollow voice. "We must stop her before she destroys our civilization."

Swampwater wagged a foamy tail.

"Stand back!" yelled Jesse. "It's a weapon!"

Next we tried Santa Claus beards and Pinocchio noses – on Swampwater and then on ourselves. It was fun – even for Swampwater. Or maybe she just liked the heat lamp.

So, yeah, as foam, Pampered Puppy was terrific. But as for removing dye … hopeless. It was sad, really, because with all that white stuff, you could almost get an idea of what the dog should look like – as Marietta, I mean. But the second we rinsed it off – Swampwater!

"This isn't working." Jesse's voice was gloomy.

"It'll take time, that's all."

Right. Time.

A hundred years or so.

This dog could grow old and *die* green.

I finished off the last Maple Critters crumbs while Jesse rubbed Swampwater dry. Then I showed him the suspect list.

LIST OF SUSPECTS

1. GAYLENE – ATHLETIC
   – LOOKING FOR ATTENTION
   – NAVY-BLUE MOUNTAIN BIKE
   – HAS KEY TO BARKING BUDDIES
2. AUSTIN – JUVENILE (EVERYTHING ABOUT HIM)
   – *EXTREMELY* CLEVER MIND
   – PAST RECORD OF PULLING PRANKS

"I just thought of something else." Jesse pointed at Austin's name. "Remember how he stared at Swampwater this morning? Remember all those questions he asked? What was *that* all about?"

"Excellent point," I said, grabbing the pen. I added another line under Austin's name:

– ASKING NOSY QUESTIONS ABOUT SWAMPWATER

I took a final glance through the list. "Only two suspects. That makes it easy. I've already started investigating Gaylene. *You* can take Austin."

"Roger." Jesse stuck out his chin and narrowed his eyes in a pretty good imitation of a private eye in an old movie. "I'll be on that guy tomorrow like a wasp on a jam sandwich."

"Good."

"Austin Alderson won't scratch his *nose* without me knowing about it."

I nodded. "Just find out if he has a bike, okay? And where he was last Sunday."

"Roger again, Stevie. I read you."

"Jesse?"

"Yeah?"

"You still reading that book? *Secret Spies and Private Eyes?"*

He frowned. "Why?"

"Nothing." I shook my head. "Good luck tomorrow."

"Roger," said Jesse.

❖ ❖ ❖

My parents were sitting down to dinner when I walked in. My mom had made some new dish with a French name. Bouillabaisse. Couldn't fool me, though. I know fish stew when I smell it.

"I thought you were starving," she said when I stood up after six bites.

I grabbed my bowl. "I'll finish it in my room."

I did, too – with a little help from Radical. From the moment I'd walked in the house, he'd been sending me grumpy cat messages. A surly look when he'd spotted Swampwater. Crabby meowing from the top of the bookshelf. Leg-clawing at the dinner table.

Fortunately, he adored bouillabaisse. As a special treat, I turned my radio to the jazz station. Radical likes all music, but his favourite is jazz, especially if there's a saxophone. He closed his eyes, stretched and purred while I stroked his neck.

After a few minutes, the news came on. When I heard the announcer say "the president," I turned it up. There was a bunch of boring stuff about the summit leaders – my dad was right, they really could talk all day about fishing rights and trade agreements. The announcer also mentioned a big banquet the leaders were having that night, featuring fresh local seafood.

"Hey, Radical! You think it's bouillabaisse?"

The next sentence made my whole body stiffen. If I'd been a dog, my ears would have perked up.

"Investigations are continuing into the disappearance of the president's Skye terrier, Marietta."

Radical let out a sour meow.

"In an interview today, the president spoke of his fondness for the little dog and his hopes that she will be recovered before he leaves Vancouver on Saturday morning. Police say they are following up on several new leads."

I jerked up so straight that Radical tumbled off my lap.

New leads? What new leads? Leads that could lead to *us?*

I listened so hard my ears hurt.

"Also in the news today, from Poland –"

As I flicked off the radio, my heart was thumping like a bass drum. All through the afternoon, first with my job and then with the dog bath, it had been easy to forget this stuff. The president. The police. The reporters. The prime minister – who I hoped had gotten some new underwear by now. Suddenly, the radio announcement made it all come crashing down again.

The police were probably out there right now, cruising the city in their squad cars, eyes peeled for any four-legged creature that looked even the slightest bit like Marietta. Dachshunds, St. Bernards, large squirrels – anything! The newspaper had said they were taking the dognapping "extremely seriously." Now the radio said they were following new leads. Maybe they had already zeroed in on a certain part of Vancouver. Like my neighbourhood, for instance. Like my street!

I caught myself just in time.

Whoa! I was as bad as Jesse. Some movie detective should smack *me* across the face and say "You're hysterical!"

Taking a long, deep breath, I stretched my neck to work out the kink I had just given myself. Then I scooped up Radical. Nothing like cuddling a soft, warm ball of fur to calm a person down. Picking up *Everything You Ever Wanted to Know About Dogs,* I started to flip through.

One of the chapter titles caught my eye. "How Dogs Communicate." A tiny flash of hope flickered through me. Swampwater knew who the Prankster was. Was it possible that she could *tell* us? Was there some way to communicate with her and find out?

I read for at least an hour. Here's what I found out: dogs have lots of different ways to communicate. Barking, for instance. They bark for all kinds of reasons – to greet you or to call you or to warn you or to ask you to play. Growling usually means the dog is angry or about to attack. Howling? That can mean loneliness, like Swampwater howling outside my bedroom door. Yelping or whimpering usually means the dog is hurt or scared.

Dogs also have all kinds of body language. Like when they sniff you – that's dog for "Who are you?" Tail-wagging is simple – it's a dog "smile." Dogs also use their posture to signal who's boss. A dog who stays low with its head and tail down is saying "Not me, man. I'm not the boss." But a dog who stands up straight, looks you in the eye, and holds its tail up – well, watch out, because that dog is about to start bossing *you* around.

Closing the book, I tried to remember how Swampwater had acted when we first found her. She'd whimpered, whined and thumped her tail. With her head hanging, she had given us sad-eyed stares. Not very hard to read *that* message. She was saying "Help!" as clearly as if she'd been able to spell it out. But as for "who done the dognapping" – well, I couldn't remember Swampwater offering any magic answers to that one.

Nope. No quick solutions from the dog. Popping the book onto my shelf, I got ready for bed. Soon I was in my bunk – with a sleeping cat below me, a dozing dog across the room, and my mind still turning over that first meeting with Swampwater. Man, she had smelled bad. My nose crinkled at the memory. All that muck.

Wait a minute …

The muck!

If Jesse and I were right, the Prankster had carried a smelly, mucky burry dog into Barking Buddies. Some of the mess *must* have gotten onto the Prankster. After all, you could still smell dirty dog in *my* backpack, even though I had wiped it out twice with a wet cloth.

I knew in a flash what Jesse and I had to do next.

Check out our suspects' clothes.

CHAPTER 10

MY DAD OFFERED ME A LIFT TO WORK THE NEXT day, and with my bike still down, I was glad to take it. Before we left, I stuck a note through Jesse's door. "Check Austin's jacket for smears and smells." It wasn't until the note had disappeared through the slot that I remembered Jesse's mother. What if *she* read it first?

I grinned, picturing Jesse as he tried to explain.

On the way to Barking Buddies, my dad talked about the money I was earning. He said he hoped I was thinking very carefully about how to spend it. Well, he got it half right. I *was* thinking very carefully.

But not about money. No, I was totally focussed on my next detective task. The muck. The smears and smells. How could I get a close look – and a good sniff – at Gaylene's jacket?

It turned out to be easy. We had just gotten the dogs settled in when a new customer showed up – a large silver-haired lady with a fancy little dog.

"I'd like a tour of the premises," she said, "to see if your establishment will be suitable for Pugsley."

Her name was Mrs. Worthington, and she was wearing a long white coat, a lot of jewellery and a big purple hat. Pugsley was her dog – a mean-looking Pekinese that she carried under one arm like a football. Personally, I've always thought Pekineses are a little weird. They look like they've had their faces punched in and wouldn't mind doing the same thing to you.

I guess Mrs. Worthington was Gaylene's dream customer because Gaylene fell all over herself trying to make a good impression. She handed over every brochure in the place and talked in this hushed, gooey voice about "the premises." Mrs. Worthington, meanwhile, kept interrupting to rattle on about the trip she and her husband – she called him Dr. Worthington – were going to take to Europe. That's why she was looking for a dog service, she said. Her housekeeper would bring Pugsley in every day, provided the day care was "suitable."

The important part is that Mrs. Worthington kept Gaylene busy. It gave me a chance to edge over to the coat rack where Gaylene had hung her jacket. Green leather. Too bad. Leather's easy to wash, so there wasn't much point looking for smears. Burrs wouldn't stick very easily either. But there was still the chance of a smell. Crouching, I stuck my nose close to the jacket and sniffed. Nothing.

Maybe I wasn't close enough. Burying my face deep in the leather, I breathed in hard.

"And what, pray tell," said Mrs. Worthington in a gravelly voice, "is *that* young person doing?"

I glanced up. Gaylene and Mrs. Worthington were staring at me.

"Stevie?" said Gaylene.

Oh boy.

"I've been reading about bloodhounds," I said, "and ..."

I had *no* idea how to finish that sentence.

Fortunately, I didn't have to. When the phone rang, I leaped over two chairs to answer it.

"Good morning. Barking Buddies!"

A man's voice. "This is Leopold Zimmer. Is Dinny there?"

"No, she – Leopold Zimmer? Really? Leopold Zimmer, the dog expert?" I almost dropped the phone. "Hey! Gaylene! It's Leopold Zimmer. I've been reading his book. Hey, Mr. Zimmer, I've got your book right here, *Everything You Ever Wanted to Know About Dogs,* and –"

That's as far as I got. Crossing the office in two steps, Gaylene snatched the phone out of my hand.

"Mr. Zimmer? I'm terribly sorry. This is Gaylene Schultz. I'm supervisor here while Dinny Barnes is on sick leave. Dinny did tell me you were coming to do more research. I am *so* looking forward to meeting you." Her voice was like honey oozing out of a jar.

I smiled at Mrs. Worthington, but she didn't smile back.

"Next Wednesday?" said Gaylene. "That would be splendid. Dinny may even be back by then. Oh, Mr. Zimmer, I can't tell you how thrilled – yes? Oh, certainly. Fine. See you then."

She hung up, looking a little dazed.

"Wow!" I said. "Leopold Zimmer! Does he live here in Vancouver?"

Gaylene nodded, tapping her forefinger absent-mindedly on the phone. "He did a lot of the research for his last book at Barking Buddies. Now he's starting a new book. It's going to be called *The Secret Language of Dogs*. He'll be here next week to do more research."

"Next week!" I let out a moan. "I'll be back at school then."

"What a shame," said Gaylene in a not-very-convincing voice.

"And he's studying dog language? Gaylene, listen, I'm really, really, *really* interested in dog language. It happens to be one of my biggest interests in the whole world right now. Are you sure he can't come sooner?"

"Stevie, you –"

"Or if he can't come sooner, maybe I could go see him. Do you have his address? Or his phone number? Can you ask him for an appointment for me?"

Gaylene held up a hand. "Stevie, please. I've never even met the man. He did his last research here long before I –"

"Hhm, hmmm." A loud clearing of the throat made us both turn. Mrs. Worthington's mouth was tight with annoyance.

"When you have a moment," she said icily.

Gaylene slapped both hands against her cheeks. "Oh, Mrs. Worthington, I'm terrible sorry. How rude of me. Please, do come this way to see our play-ground."

I was still thinking about Leopold Zimmer as I followed them into Pooch Playground, so I didn't really see what happened. All I knew for sure was that Brutus seemed to take an instant dislike to Pugsley. Well, okay, Pugsley was a nasty little thing – even the purple bows in his hair couldn't hide that. Still, I wasn't sure why Brutus would lunge at him that way, snarling and growling. Pugsley was still safely out of reach in Mrs. Worthington's armpit, but I guess *he* didn't think he was high enough because he started trying to climb up on top of her hat. Swampwater had joined in the racket, yipping along with her big buddy, Brutus. And Mrs. Worthington? She was doing some yipping of her own. It can't be much fun having a dog climb your face.

All in all, it was pretty exciting. It didn't last long, though. Within seconds, Gaylene had a death grip on Brutus's collar and was hauling him out of the way. Mrs. Worthington flapped around for a few more minutes, trying to straighten her hat, which had gone one way, and her glasses, which had been knocked another. She was gasping and muttering at me and Gaylene, and it was hard to make out the words, but "outrageous" was definitely one of them. Also, "deplorable" and "insufferable." Gaylene tried to calm her down, but it was no use. Clutching Pugsley protectively, Mrs. Worthington staggered back to the office and out into the street.

"Well!" Gaylene was practically pop-eyed. "You really did it this time, Stevie Diamond."

"Me!" I said. "What did *I* do?"

According to Gaylene, plenty. The whole thing ended up being my fault, mostly because of Swampwater. Gaylene insisted – can you believe this? – that it was Swampwater who had caused the problem between Brutus and Pugsley. The little green dog was a troublemaker, said Gaylene. What's more, she had talked to Dinny the night before, and Dinny said I didn't even *have* a dog. So who was this ugly little mongrel anyway?

"She's a stray, isn't she?" Gaylene was breathing heavily, getting more worked up every second. "Well, let me tell you something, Stevie Diamond. Barking Buddies is a business, and while Dinny is away, it's *my* business. As acting supervisor, I cannot accept responsibility for stray dogs – especially mangy little mongrels that are totally undisciplined. That dog does *not* belong here. She belongs in the pound!"

She reached out with both hands to grab Swampwater.

CHAPTER 11

I've seen at least five movies where someone threatens to take a dog to the pound, so I knew *exactly* what to do.

I grabbed Swampwater and clutched her to my chest. "No!" I cried in one of those scared-but-brave voices kids use in the movies. "You can't! I won't let you!"

I must have done a pretty good job. Either that, or Gaylene had seen the same movies. Her hands twitched for a moment before dropping slowly to her sides. She took a few more noisy breaths. Then, shoulders stiff, she edged over to the desk.

But that didn't mean she forgave Swampwater. Or me. Oh no, I was definitely in the doghouse. I mean, I was in *a* dog house – a building full of dogs – but I was also in *the* doghouse with Gaylene. Figuring this out, I almost giggled. Too bad I didn't have someone to share the joke with.

Gaylene?

Not a chance.

The rest of the morning was rough. Gaylene and I walked the dogs together, but she wasn't exactly speaking to me, so I had to solve my *own* dog problems. Dagwood, for one. Shep wasn't there, so it was up to me to control a huge puppy who had about as much sense of direction as a chicken. In fact, if I'd had a choice – Dagwood or chicken – I would definitely have picked the chicken. I spent the whole morning pulling Dagwood out of garbage cans, gutters and flower beds. By eleven o'clock, my arms were aching all the way up to my neck.

I didn't let it affect my brain, though. The whole time we were walking, I was thinking, mostly about the way Gaylene had acted after the Mrs. Worthington disaster. Why had she blamed Swampwater and threatened her with the pound? After all, it was Brutus who had caused the problem. Unless …

Maybe Gaylene never intended to take Swampwater to the pound at all. Maybe it was just a way for her – if she *was* the Prankster – to get her hands back on the president's dog. Yeah. Maybe she'd been *waiting* for an excuse to grab the dog back. I watched her out of the corner of my eye, but her face was as empty as a school yard during spring break. If there were any clues there, *I* sure couldn't see them.

I ate my lunch on the front-office couch. Gaylene ate hers at the desk. We didn't speak. I read a six-month-old copy of *Dog Breeders' Digest*. Gaylene skipped around in a book called *The A to Z of Canine Disease*. It was grim.

At one o'clock, Gaylene told me I could walk some dogs on my own that afternoon.

"I need a break," she said. She didn't say "from you," but I could tell that was what she meant. "Take Lulu, Walter and Dagwood."

"And Swampwater," I added quickly.

She sighed.

Wondering if I was pushing my luck, I blurted out, "Do I have to take Dagwood?"

"Well, I can't walk *two* untrained dogs, Stevie." Gaylene's voice was definitely irritated. "I'll already have Brutus to deal with."

"Oh." I thought hard. Really, truly, I couldn't stand another hour of Dagwood.

"How about if *I* take Brutus?" At least he walked in the right direction.

"Brutus?" Gaylene stared. "Are you serious?"

"I can do it," I insisted. Through the front window, I spotted Jesse locking up his bike. "Look! Jesse's here. He can help."

Gaylene shook her head. She said I didn't have the strength or the experience to handle Brutus. But when Jesse offered to walk a couple of the dogs for me, she started to waver.

"Well …"

I dashed into Pooch Playground before she had a chance to change her mind.

❖ ❖ ❖

Jesse took Lulu and Walter. I walked Swampwater and Brutus. The dogs started at a run, as usual, so for the first block we didn't get much chance to talk.

I hung on to the leash knot carefully and kept a sharp eye on Brutus. The big shepherd was strong, all right, but it was a relief to have just two dogs. It helped, too, that they were both smart enough to move in the same direction.

On our second block, we slowed down. We crossed Burrard Street easily – a surprise. Usually, it's tough to get across with a bunch of dogs, but today the traffic was light.

"What are you doing here?" I asked Jesse first chance I got. "I thought you were going to tail Austin today."

His face turned glum. "Austin spotted me. I followed him into his math camp, and I *thought* I had a good hiding spot, but ..."

"What was the hiding spot?"

"Under a desk."

"What's wrong with that?"

"Turned out to be the teacher's desk."

"Bad luck," I said.

Jesse nodded. "I had to do some fast talking. I said I was interested in the camp. They showed me around and made me read a bunch of brochures. I even did a math placement test." He shuddered. "On spring break."

"So you didn't find out anything?"

"Sure I did. I spotted something important."

"What?"

Just then we had to stop to let Lulu take a bathroom break. I showed Jesse the plastic bags.

"What? No! I quit!"

"Calm down, Jesse. I'll do it. Tell me what you spotted."

"Austin bought a newspaper."

"So?"

"So I watched him. He didn't really read it at all. He just glanced through it – like he was looking for something special. I saw him zero right in on the bottom of page eight."

"So?" I said again. Dropping the plastic bag into a garbage can, I motioned Jesse to cross Cornwall. It was easy – there were no cars. None. Zero. Boy, the traffic really *was* light.

"I bought a copy of the newspaper," continued Jesse. "Guess what's at the bottom of page eight."

"What?"

"An article about the president's dog."

"You're kidding! And Austin went straight for it?"

Jesse nodded. "Didn't even look at the comics."

"Whoa." I shivered. "That's bizarre."

"It's not bizarre at all. It's exactly what the Prankster would do. Right?"

The Prankster? Skinny little Austin?

We stepped aside for a woman pushing a double stroller with two identical red-headed babies in it. One was slumped over asleep, cracker crumbs all over its face, but the other one started bouncing with excitement when it saw the dogs.

"What did the article say, Jesse?"

"It said something really scary. It said the police have some new leads. What leads, Stevie? Leads to who? How?"

His shoulders were creeping up towards his ears. Uh-oh. Pretty soon he'd be talking about walking to Mexico.

"Don't worry," I told him. "I heard the same thing on the radio last night. They *always* say that. It's one of those things police say."

His voice turned hopeful. "You think so?"

"Yep."

"You're sure it's not … like … leads to *us?*"

I shrugged and gestured around. "You see any police?"

Jesse stopped. He looked around in all directions. "Stevie?"

"Yeah?"

"You notice anything … weird?"

I stopped, too. Gazed around. Jesse was right. The street looked … odd. Different. Bare.

"Where are the cars?" asked Jesse.

He was right. There were *no* cars. Not even parked ones. It was as if a fleet of tow trucks had come along and hauled away every vehicle they could find.

I pointed at the nearest intersection. "Where's the mailbox, Jesse?"

"Stevie?"

"There's supposed to be a mailbox right there."

"Stevie?"

"I *know* it was there. I stuck a letter in it last week."

"STEVIE!" This time he yelled it, right in my ear. "LOOK!"

Suddenly, I felt like I was in one of those weird movies about the future. A big city street – bare, except for a few little knots of people standing on the sidewalk. Waiting. Staring at the same thing – a row of headlights. Advancing slowly towards us with a dull roar of motors.

Motorcycles! Four of them. Big ones. Their riders were all in black, wearing huge helmets.

Jesse's fingers dug into my right arm. "Cops!" he blurted. "They're coming for *me,* Stevie! Oh no, oh no, oh no, oh mommy, mommy, mommy …"

I couldn't calm him down. I couldn't reassure him. Those motorcycles *were* coming straight for us. And there were four more behind them … and then four more. Rows and rows of them.

Geez! How many police did it *take* to arrest two twelve-year-old kids?

Have you ever had one of those dreams where

something really terrible is about to happen, and you know you should do something – scream maybe, or run away – but nothing in your whole body works? You can't move, you can't speak, you can hardly even breathe?

That was me and Jesse, frozen to the pavement like a couple of lampposts. The dogs snuffled and whimpered around our ankles. Even *they* could tell something was wrong.

The motorcycles were close enough for us to see the gleaming chrome. The roar of motors was thick and heavy in our ears. If there had been a moment to run away, it was already past. I could see the police clearly now – the white helmets, the black boots, the gloves, the dark sunglasses that hid their eyes. And if I could see *them,* then they could see *us.* Two kids, quivering on the sidewalk. A bunch of dogs. One of them little and green.

And stolen.

Oh, mommy, mommy, mommy …

Jesse's eyes were closed. His lips were moving, but nothing was coming out. He was holding on to the leash knot, but both his hands were high above his head.

Surrender!

Good idea.

My hands were high above my head, too, as the first four motorcycles rolled past. Yup, rolled past. They drove up to where Jesse and I were standing with the dogs – and they kept right on going.

Then came the next four. They rolled past, too, the riders staring straight ahead like zombies. Then four more. Right past again.

I lowered my arms. "Jesse, look!"

Eyes still squeezed shut, mouth clamped tight, he shook his head fiercely.

Down the street – where the motorcycles had first appeared – something else was going on. I stared. More motorcycles, and then some cars. Big black fancy shiny ones. As they came closer, I could see people inside. Guys in suits.

"Hey, Jesse, check this out."

Face pale, eyes closed tight, Jesse shook his head again.

Then I saw a limousine – with a Canadian flag on the front … a big, red maple leaf. The little knots of people on the sidewalk started clapping. Finally, I got it. The summit!

"Jesse! It's the prime minister. Open your eyes."

As the prime minister's limousine rolled by, I saw his face really clearly. He actually waved to me and smiled. He looked like *such* a nice guy. Gosh! I hoped he'd managed to get some new underwear.

Jesse had one eye open as the second limo purred past. The flag on this one was the Japanese rising sun. Oh wow! I waved, but the men inside were talking, so I didn't get a wave back.

And then, on the next limo, I saw the stars and stripes. It was him – the American president! Now, I know this may be hard to believe, but I was so excited I didn't even *remember* that I was walking his stolen dog. I just stood there, grinning and waving like an idiot, hoping he would wave back.

He waved to some people on our side of the street, but just before his limo reached us, he turned to wave at people on the other side. I saw the back of his head and his silvery hair and his raised hand. Then – whoosh – he was gone.

More limos went by after that, but I couldn't tell you who was in them. That's because the second the president's limousine went by, Swampwater went berserk. She started barking frantically, leaping around and jerking on her leash. She was trying to follow him!

Well, it *would* have been all right. I mean, I *could* have held on to Swampwater – if it hadn't been for Brutus. Yes sir, that German shepherd was definitely in love. He was a one-dog fan club for the little green mutt, and if *she* was going to bark and jerk and pull – well, so was he. I grabbed the leash knot with both hands and yelled.

"Jesse! Help!"

But by then it was a chain reaction. I don't think Lulu and Walter had any idea what the fuss was about, but the next thing we knew, *they* were leaping and pulling and barking, too.

"I *can't* help!" Jesse yelled back.

So there I was, solo, in a tug of war with Brutus and Swampwater. I held on for a long time, trying to grip the sidewalk with my running shoes, but I knew I was in trouble when I felt the soles sliding along and the heat coming up through the rubber. I got dragged half a block that way. Finally, I wrapped myself around a fire hydrant and tried to wrap the leashes around it, too, but no. The dogs had pulled them too tight. That Brutus – man, he was strong! He was pulling my arms right out of their shoulder sockets. He was separating my hands from my arms at the wrists. The leash knot was damp from my sweaty hands. I could feel it slipping, slipping ...

And then –

They were gone!

I dropped onto the sidewalk with a thud. The huge German shepherd and the little green mutt disappeared at greyhound speed down the half-empty street. The leash knot bobbed up and down between them like a bouncing ball.

CHAPTER 12

THIS TIME JESSE COULDN'T GO AFTER THE RUNAWAYS. He was having too much trouble with Lulu and Walter. I leaped to my feet and grabbed Lulu's collar.

It took a few minutes to settle the poodle and the beagle down. Long enough for the whole parade, or whatever it was, to end. Jesse collapsed against the window of a grocery store.

"Oh, wow, Stevie, that was –" He glanced around, bewildered. "Where's Swampwater? And Brutus?"

"Gone."

Jesse's eyes bugged out. "Which way did they go?"

Feeling sick, I pointed.

"Come on, Stevie. What are we waiting for?"

I shook my head. "They're blocks away by now."

Stunned, Jesse stared at Lulu and Walter. They looked a lot calmer. Walter even flopped down onto his belly, as if all that excitement had worn him out.

"What are we going to tell Gaylene?" asked Jesse.

I winced. Right. Gaylene.

She had told me I wasn't strong or experienced enough to handle Brutus. When she found out he was gone, she'd go nuts. And what about Swamp-water? If Gaylene *wasn't* the Prankster, she wouldn't care if the little green dog disappeared off the planet. But if she *was,* and I'd lost her stolen prize ... well, she'd be ready to dye me green, stuff me in a broom closet, and throw away the key. Forever.

Somewhere in my stomach, there was a knot that said I probably deserved it.

"Stick around," I begged Jesse. "Please? This could be rough."

He gulped. Then he nodded. I grabbed the leashes, and we headed back to Barking Buddies – really slowly.

❖ ❖ ❖

The door was locked. I knocked, but there was no answer.

"She must be out walking the other dogs." Relief flooded through me. Silly, I know. I'd have to face her sooner or later. But give me a choice between sooner and later, and I'll pick later every time – especially if it involves someone yelling at me. I found Dinny's key in my backpack and let us in.

A few minutes later, Jesse and I were tossing tennis balls for Walter and Lulu in Pooch Playground when there was a sharp knock at the front door.

"Who's that?" asked Jesse

I peered at my watch. "Too early for the owners. I'll go check."

The guy at the door was wearing a grey suit, with a long beige coat hanging open over top. He had thick brown hair, a clipped brown moustache and a wide nose that looked like it might have been broken in some long-ago fight. His shoulders were football-player size and so was his chest. Even though it was cloudy out, he was wearing a pair of silver-rimmed sunglasses – the mirrored kind.

This was *not* a Barking Buddies customer.

"Yes?" I said, straightening my shoulders and trying to look a few years older. Like maybe thirty.

Flipping open a little leather case, he flashed a gold badge at me. "Special Agent Deke Rifkin. I'm on assignment with the president of the United States. Can I talk with you for a minute? It's about a lost dog."

This was it.

It was actually happening.

If I could have wished myself off to some faraway place – Africa, say, or Antarctica – I would have done it. Even if I couldn't come back for ten years. Or even twenty. I would have done it, I swear.

"Can I come in?" asked Special Agent Rifkin a moment later, when I still hadn't said anything.

Behind me, I heard a shaky voice. "Stevie? Who's that?"

I took a deep breath and licked my lips. Good. My tongue still worked.

"It's … uh, Special Agent Rifkin," I said over my shoulder in a strange, raspy voice I didn't recognize. "He wants to, um, talk to us about … about a dog."

"This will just take a minute," said Agent Rifkin, stepping inside. "You are?"

"Stevie Diamond," I said, still in that weird voice. "And this is …" For a moment, I couldn't remember. "Oh yeah, Jesse Kulniki."

Eyes wide, Jesse nodded his head up and down rapidly. "I don't have a dog," he said. "Never had a dog. No dog at all. My mom's allergic."

Agent Rifkin smiled – a little jerk of his mouth muscles that widened his lips for a second before they snapped back into place. "We're just following up a few leads," he said.

Leads. Oh boy.

Agent Rifkin reached inside his coat and pulled out a notebook and a pen.

"Mind if I sit down?" Without waiting for an answer, he sat on the couch. At the top of the page, in precise, careful handwriting, he wrote the date. Then he wrote some other stuff I couldn't make out, since it was upside down, but I *did* see my name: Stevie Diamond.

Oh boy.

Jesse peeked over my shoulder. He must have seen his name, too, because he turned worm white.

"We're following up on reports about a dog that we believe might be in your possession," said Agent Rifkin, still writing.

"Dog?" I tried to smile. "This place is full of dogs. Usually. Right now, most of them are out walking."

Agent Rifkin did that fake-smile thing with his lips again. "This is a very special dog," he said. "A little cream-coloured dog. At least, it *was* cream-coloured. We have reason to believe that the dog's colour may have been altered."

"Altered?" squeaked Jesse.

"Let's get to the point." Reaching inside his coat again, Rifkin pulled out a newspaper clipping. He held it up so that we could see it. It was the picture of Swampwater on the president's lap. "Do you recognize this dog?"

"Well … not exactly," I said.

"Sort of," added Jesse. "Maybe just a little."

Agent Rifkin made an impatient-sounding noise. "Look, kids. I need a straight answer here."

"Well …" I said again. "We *did* have a dog that looked maybe a *little* bit like that one. But we don't have it any more."

Jesse nodded, then shrugged. "It's gone."

"Gone?" repeated Agent Rifkin.

"We … um, lost it," I told him. "Today. We also lost another dog. They ran away together."

The muscles in Agent Rifkin's jaw tightened. "You're sure?"

I nodded. "I tried to hold on to their leashes, but …"

Agent Rifkin let his breath out in a long sigh. Then he shook his head, almost sadly. "You seem like nice kids," he said. "I hate to see nice kids get into so much trouble."

Was it my imagination, or did he drag the words out? Sooooooo muuuuuuch.

"T-trouble?" stammered Jesse.

"That is a *very* important dog," said Rifkin.

Jesse's eyes flitted around the room. "What if – what if we find it?" His panic-stricken glance settled on me. "Stevie and I – we can find the dog. Can't we, Stevie?"

The only answer I could think of was "Are you nuts?" It seemed wiser to keep my mouth shut.

"Yeah, sure, no problem," Jesse continued, talking really fast. "I mean, it's probably not the right dog or anything. I mean, you're probably – ha ha – barking up the wrong tree. But if you want to see that dog, well, sir, we'll just find it for you. Yes, sir, we will. Absolutely!"

Rifkin grunted. One thick brown eyebrow rose above the silver frame of his sunglasses. Closing his notebook, the special agent heaved himself up off the couch.

"Well, son," he said, gazing down at Jesse. "I hope you're right. Because I'll tell you something – I'm going to have to come back here. And next time, well … I won't be alone. So you know what I'd do if I were you?"

Jesse shook his head.

Agent Rifkin stuffed his notebook back inside his coat. He adjusted his watch, picked a small piece of lint off his sleeve, and strode towards the door. Then he turned. I could see our tiny, skinny reflections in his sunglasses.

"I'd try very, very hard to find that dog."

CHAPTER

As soon as Special Agent Rifkin was gone, Jesse fell onto the couch, groaning and clutching his stomach.

"Stevie, I can't take this. I quit. I don't even want to *be* a detective any more."

"No? Then why did you tell Rifkin we could find Swampwater? How, exactly, are we supposed to do that?"

"I don't know, I don't know, I don't know." Jesse was rolling back and forth like someone who's been punched. "I just wanted him to leave. I would have said anything."

"Well, what do we do when he comes back? You heard him. He's coming back – with more police."

Jesse gave me an agonized look. "Mexico. It's the only way, Stevie."

Mexico was suddenly looking good.

I don't know how long Jesse and I sat there, but I *do* know that we said a lot of stupid things. Some of them started with "It was your fault that," and others started with "If only you hadn't," and the worst ones started with "Well I think you're a big." It was *not* fun, and I was almost grateful when I heard a bunch of thuds, rustles and whines at the front door. Gaylene and the dogs.

Get it over with quickly, I told myself as they walked in. I stood up and faced Gaylene.

"It's about Brutus and Swampwater," I blurted.

Gaylene was fiddling with her leash knot and barely looked up. "What about them?"

"They're gone."

"Gone where?"

"Just gone."

Gaylene glanced up from the tangled leash knot, one eyebrow arched. "What is this, Stevie? More nonsense? Brutus is out back. I can hear him, for heaven's sake!"

"No, Gaylene, really, I –"

I stopped. Behind Gaylene, Jesse was standing on the couch making wild, crazy faces. He mouthed something I couldn't make out and pointed towards Pooch Playground.

Then I heard it. The deep "rrrruu-rrruu-rruuff" that belonged to only one dog in the day care. Brutus! It was coming from the playground. I turned and walked – I could barely stop myself from running – toward the sound. Jesse was right behind me.

I couldn't see Brutus, but sitting there, panting and wagging her tail, right beside Walter and Lulu, was Swampwater. When she saw me, she ran forward but got stopped by the leash.

The leash! What was it tied to? I followed it to a spot at the bottom of the high wooden fence. What? The leash ran underneath one of the boards – and a deep "ruuuffff" was coming from the other side.

"Brutus is out in the lane, Jesse," I hissed. "Their leashes are still tied together."

"Yeah, but how did Swampwater get inside?" he hissed back.

I grabbed the board that the leash ran under and pulled on it. The board was loose. Not so loose that it pulled right off, or even so loose that a large German shepherd could fit through – this explained why Brutus was still on the other side. But it was loose enough for a little green terrier to push her way through. And then, it was tight enough to snap back into place. Looking at the board now, it was impossible to tell that it had been moved – until you saw the leash.

"Will you look at that!" said Jesse. "A secret entrance."

"Quick!" I said. "Run around back. Untie Brutus and bring him in the front. I'll distract Gaylene."

Distracting Gaylene wasn't that tough. I just insisted on showing her something in the storage room. I looked a little silly when it turned out to be a package of dog toothbrushes that had broken open. But it was worth it when, over Gaylene's shoulder, I spotted Jesse sneaking Brutus past the door.

A giggle bubbled up in me. I tried to stop it, but only managed to re-route it – through my nose. Gaylene stared, eyebrows furrowed, as I snorted. The sound made me laugh – or rather, snort – even harder.

Gaylene rolled her eyes. When I didn't stop, she shook her head and left. I fell against a wall, still laughing.

No doubt about it.

This case was *getting* to me.

❖ ❖ ❖

Jesse left for a guitar lesson soon after. We didn't get a chance to talk until later that evening, in his bathroom, hunched over a soggy, sudsy dog.

"So what do you think it means, Stevie?" Jesse was working up a thick lather on Swampwater's neck. "That secret entrance to the Barking Buddies yard?"

Before I could say anything, he answered his own question.

"It means Swampwater could have gotten into the yard all by herself, right? On the day she was stolen?"

I nodded and worked the shampoo into a particularly green spot on Swampwater's back.

"We have to think it all through again," I said. "Here's how it *could* have happened. The Prankster grabs Swampwater in Stanley Park and rides away on his bike. Then somehow he loses her."

Jesse grunted. "No problem there. The dog's an escape artist. *We've* already lost her twice."

"So the dog escapes," I continued, "and – hey, this could explain the way Swampwater looked – she runs through some burry plants and muck."

"And she rolls in it," said Jesse, wrinkling his nose.

"Right. She rolls in it, and she keeps going, and after a while she's wandering down a back lane and – and maybe she smells a bunch of doggy smells coming from behind a fence!"

"Yeah," said Jesse. "Doggy smells! So she sniffs

around and finds a loose board, and she pushes her way in and – bang! – she's trapped in the Barking Buddies yard."

A smile curled the corners of his mouth. I smiled back. Yes. It was *totally* possible.

As if she knew we were talking about her, Swampwater stood on her hind legs against the side of the tub and barked. Soapy smears dripped over onto the floor.

"Down, girl." Jesse pushed the dog's front legs back into the tub and started to rinse her off with a plastic cup.

I grabbed another cup to help, still thinking hard. "This means that the Prankster might never have come anywhere *near* Barking Buddies. It also means that you and I may never have come anywhere near the Prankster."

Jesse frowned. "Maybe. But you know what, Stevie? There's something that keeps bugging me."

"What's that?"

"Your bike tire."

I stopped rinsing. My bike tire? What did *that* have to do with anything?

"Think about it," Jesse continued. "Don't you think it's a little suspicious that your tire got a huge slash in it just one day after we found the president's dog?"

"What –" Suddenly I got it. "You think somebody slashed my tire on purpose?"

Jesse shrugged. "It's possible."

I put down my cup. "Jesse! I just thought of something. Remember how Swampwater barked and woke everyone up in the middle of the night on Monday? Well, maybe she *heard* something.

Yeah, sure, dogs have terrific hearing. So maybe she heard somebody out there in the courtyard – slashing my bike tire."

Jesse nodded. "Somebody known as the Prankster. The only problem is – why? What good would it do the Prankster to slash your bike tire?"

We both thought for a moment. Then, with a suddenness that made Swampwater jump, I clapped my hands. "It would stop me from riding my bike. It would make me *walk* to work with Swampwater! That's it, don't you see? I'm an easier target on foot."

Another memory flashed through my brain.

"JESSE!" I yelled it so loud that Swampwater did a wild leap, splashing soapy water all over Jesse.

"What the – what are you doing?" snapped Jesse as he grabbed the dog. Water sloshed over his wrists and up his arms.

"The woman with the baby carriage! And the baby named Lawrence!"

Jesse was elbow deep in scummy water now, wrestling with the thrashing dog. The front of his grey sweatshirt was soaked through.

"She ran me down! She knocked me over! Jesse, will you please *stop* that?" I grabbed Swampwater, hauled her out of the tub, and threw a fluffy white towel around her.

"Not that towel," said Jesse. "That's my mom's best –"

"Jesse, *listen* to me!" I snatched a handful of wet sweatshirt, jerked him towards me, and stared into his eyes. "I think that woman with the baby might have been the Prankster!"

"Stevie! For crying out loud, I just bought this

shirt." Pulling my hand away, he smoothed the wrinkled lump I had made. "Anyway, don't you think you're getting a little carried away? How could Baby Lawrence's mom be doing all this stuff – riding mountain bikes, pushing basketball players into closets – when she has a little baby to take care of?"

"Did you *see* Baby Lawrence?" I asked. "I never saw Baby Lawrence."

"But I thought you said –"

"A baby carriage, Jesse. I saw the carriage. But I never saw one single toe of Baby Lawrence. And hey! I never *heard* him either – even though I did a somersault right over top of him."

"You mean –"

I nodded. "Maybe there *was* no Baby Lawrence."

"An empty baby carriage?" Jesse's eyes widened. "Oooh, Stevie. That's too creepy."

Swampwater scampered out of her towel and dashed over to Jesse, where she stood with her head cocked to one side and her tongue hanging out. Jesse gathered her up in his arms.

"There's only one thing that doesn't fit," I said after a moment.

"What's that?"

"If Baby Lawrence's mom is the Prankster, why did she stop?"

"Stop what?"

"Stop trying to get the dog back. That *must* be what she was trying to do on Tuesday when she crashed into me. But we haven't seen her since. It doesn't make sense."

"Exactly," said Jesse. He reached into the tub and pulled the plug. "We never saw her again. So maybe she's *not* the Prankster. Maybe it was just a coincidence that you crashed into her the day after your tire got slashed."

"Maybe." Now I was totally confused.

"Anyway," said Jesse, "you're forgetting all that evidence I gathered on Austin. The newspaper? Page eight? The dog article?"

Good point. Austin was still high on our list of suspects. The guy was acting really nervous – more than Jesse even knew. Picking up Brutus that day, Austin had been flushed and sweaty. He wouldn't look me in the eye. He seemed to be in a big hurry to leave, too, but when I came outside fifteen minutes later, he was still there, watching me and Swampwater from behind a parked van.

"Austin's not acting normal," I agreed. "You'd better stay on his trail."

Jesse nodded. "I've already got a plan. You know Matthew Rigby? That guy I shared a locker with last year? Well, he and Austin are best friends now."

True. Austin and Matthew spent huge amounts of time together, mostly in the computer lab.

"Think I'll pay a visit to old Matthew tomorrow." Jesse's jaw muscles clenched, and his eyes went all squinty. "See what *he* knows."

"See if you can find out what kind of bicycle Austin has," I suggested. "And Jesse? Be careful. Don't let him know why you're asking."

Jesse made a zipper-closing movement over his lips. Then he stuck his head into the bathroom cupboard and started pulling out cleansers and sponges. Hmmm ... this looked like an excellent time to bring our suspect list up to date. Taking the paper out of my pocket, I started writing.

Ten minutes later, the tub was clean (Jesse), and the list was up to date (me). The tub looked brand-new. The list looked like this:

LIST OF SUSPECTS

1. GAYLENE – ATHLETIC
– LOOKING FOR ATTENTION
– NAVY-BLUE MOUNTAIN BIKE
– HAS KEY TO BARKING BUDDIES

2. AUSTIN – JUVENILE (EVERYTHING ABOUT HIM)
– *EXTREMELY* CLEVER MIND
– PAST RECORD OF PULLING PRANKS
– ASKING NOSY QUESTIONS ABOUT SWAMPWATER
– READING DOG ARTICLE IN NEWSPAPER
– ACTING NERVOUS/SPYING

3. BABY LAWRENCE'S MOM
– CONNECTED TO SLASHED TIRE?
– WAS THE CRASH REALLY AN ACCIDENT?
– IS THERE REALLY A BABY LAWRENCE?

"Looks good," muttered Jesse after he'd read the list.

"Wish I could say the same thing about the dog," I said. Swampwater was sniffing my foot.

"Don't you think she's maybe a *little* better?" asked Jesse. "A little faded? I mean, you wouldn't really call that colour swampwater green any more, would you?

"Well, not exactly."

"She's not green at all," said Jesse eagerly. "She's more like ..."

There was a pause.

"Puke yellow," I said.

It was true. The dog was now the awful brownish yellow colour of a recycled meal.

Jesse groaned. "This is *never* going to end, is it? We're going to spend our whole lives this way – on the run, hiding out, dodging the police. We're going to keep washing this dumb dog till our fingers shrivel up. This is never, ever, *ever* going to end."

I thought about Special Agent Rifkin. A shiver wriggled up my spine.

"It could end a lot sooner than you think," I said.

Jesse gulped. "Rifkin?"

I nodded. "He'll be back. Maybe even tomorrow."

Jesse stared down at the scruffy yellow dog. His shoulders sagged. Swampwater still looked about as much like Marietta as I look like Santa Claus.

"What we need now," said Jesse glumly, "is a miracle."

CHAPTER 14

STANDING OUTSIDE THE DOOR TO BARKING BUDDIES the next morning, I remembered Jesse's words. Miracles do happen, I reminded myself as I pushed the door open. At least, in movies and books they do.

But there was no miracle waiting at Barking Buddies. Only Gaylene Schultz, talking to Dagwood's owner – a round-faced guy with big puppy-dog eyes who laughed a lot, at anything.

"Morning, Stevie." Gaylene peered at her watch, but I knew I was on time. "Could you go out to the playground, dear, and do a quick clean-up? Dagwood had a little accident back there." She smiled a plummy-lipped smile at Dagwood's owner.

"I just don't know what to *do* with that dog," he said, chuckling merrily.

I've got a few ideas, I thought, as I headed to the playground. After cleaning up the mess, I came back to the office. Dagwood's owner was gone, and the phone was ringing. Gaylene got it.

"Good morning. Barking Buddies. Yes. Oh, Mr. Zimmer, it's you. What? Today? Why, certainly. We'd be thrilled. Oh yes, absolutely!"

Gaylene's eyes were bright, her cheeks flushed, as she hung up. "Oh my goodness. We – oh heavens, look at this place. Stevie, quickly! Help me tidy up. Leopold Zimmer is coming."

"The dog author? I thought he was coming *next* week."

"Something's come up." Gaylene started bouncing around the office like a Ping-Pong ball, picking things up and putting them down. "He has to go to Toronto next week. He'll be here in twenty minutes. Oh, will you look at this. Dog tracks all over the floor. Stevie, can you get the mop, please?"

I figured that a dog expert like Leopold Zimmer had probably *seen* dog tracks before, but I didn't argue. I found the mop in the storage room and wiped up the tracks. I also straightened the papers on Gaylene's desk and dusted the lamps and furniture. The whole time, I was thinking –

It's happening! My miracle! Leopold Zimmer's next book – the one he planned to research at Barking Buddies – was *The Secret Language of Dogs*. What could be more perfect? This guy spoke dog.

Maybe he could talk to Swampwater. Or, at least, *listen* to her. Maybe he could find out what really happened last Sunday and get Jesse and me off the hook.

I couldn't believe our luck! Here we were, at the very end of our rope, and who comes along? Only the best possible person in the whole city, that's all. A dog expert.

By the time the front door opened half an hour later, it was hard to tell who was more thrilled – me or Gaylene. Gaylene did all the talking, of course.

"Oh, Mr. Zimmer, I can't *tell* you how pleased we are. We were going to take the dogs out for a walk, but when we learned that we'd have your company, we put our schedule aside and ..."

I won't bore you with the rest. Just imagine a skinny, excited dog, slurping its tongue, wagging its tail, and you'll get an idea of how Gaylene was acting. I, meanwhile, was studying Leopold Zimmer. I'd never seen a miracle before.

He was younger than I expected – about thirty – with sandy-coloured hair. His front teeth stuck out, just a little. He wore faded blue jeans, a white shirt, a nubbly wool vest, and a scruffy-looking tweed sports jacket. A pair of rimless glasses perched on the bridge of his nose.

His smile was friendly, even if it was a bit toothy, and he was nodding cheerfully at Gaylene as if he agreed with every word she said. And, believe me, she said a *lot* of words. After what felt like twenty minutes, she finally introduced me.

I decided to be cool. "I've got your book right here, Mr. Zimmer, and I'm really enjoying it."

"That's wonderful." Leopold Zimmer shook my hand enthusiastically. "I always enjoy meeting one of my readers."

"Would you like to see the dogs now?" Gaylene motioned towards Pooch Playground. "I'd be honoured if you'd come along with us on our walk today, Mr. Zimmer."

"Call me Leo," he said, holding up a hand and including me in his smile. "So much friendlier."

I darted a look at Gaylene. Maybe *Ms. Schultz* could learn a thing or two from Call-me-Leo. But she was already on her way to the playground.

I was about to follow when the phone rang. Gaylene glanced back.

"Stevie, dear? Can you get that?"

She and Leopold disappeared. I grabbed the phone on the third ring.

"Stevie?" said a female voice. "This is Dinny."

"Oh, Dinny, hi. How's your grape– I mean, your knee?"

"Much better. I'm not up for dog-walking yet, but I *am* off the crutches and feeling a lot more energetic. In fact, I thought I'd drop in later and see how things are going. Is Gaylene there?"

"She's with Leopold Zimmer," I said.

"Leopold? I thought he wasn't coming till next week."

I told her about the trip to Toronto.

"What a shame," said Dinny. "I'll be sorry to miss him. But what am I saying? He should be around for the rest of the day. Tell him and Gaylene I'll be there in an hour and a half. Stevie? What's that noise?"

Growls, wild noisy yips, and deep rrruu-rrruuff barks were coming from the playground. I recognized the yips – Swampwater. And the barks.

"Brutus," I said.

Dinny made a huffing noise. "I *knew* we shouldn't have taken that dog in before he was properly trained. I explained – oh, never mind, Stevie, it's not your problem. Tell Gaylene we'll discuss Brutus when I get there."

"Okay," I said. "See you later, Dinny. Bye."

In the playground, Gaylene was huddled in a corner, giving Brutus the king-sized, super-duper, heavy-duty Top Dog treatment. Her dark eyes flashed as she eyeballed the German shepherd, and she scolded him in a voice that was so crisp, it practically crackled. Her grip on his collar was white-knuckled, and if that dog wasn't getting the message that Gaylene was alpha, well, there had to be something seriously wrong with him. *I* sure wouldn't have argued with her.

A *wolf* wouldn't have argued with her.

Brutus acted pretty dumb at times, but I guess underneath it all, he had enough German shepherd brains to know he should stop annoying Gaylene. With a whimper of submission, he lay down at her feet.

"Are you all right, Mr. – Leo?" Gaylene's voice turned to butter. "I'm terribly sorry. Brutus has been acting up all week. He's enrolled in obedience school next week, or we wouldn't even have him here."

"Perfectly all right," said Leopold Zimmer, brushing dust off the backside of his jeans. "Understandable, too. I'm a stranger, and I'm sure I have the smell of my two rottweilers on me."

"Anthony and Cleopatra," I said. Leopold Zimmer mentioned his rottweilers a lot in *Everything You Ever Wanted to Know About Dogs*.

He smiled that sweet toothy smile. "My! You *have* been reading my book."

"You bet!" I said. "I'm especially interested in the part about communication, and I was wondering if –"

"Stevie?" Gaylene's voice was getting a little crackly again. "If you have any questions, could you ask Mr. Zimmer later, please? It's time to leash your dogs."

"Oh yeah. Sure."

Gaylene and I leashed the dogs while Leopold Zimmer wrote some stuff in a hardbacked notebook with spiral rings at the top. I tried to get a peek, but all I could make out was a few lines of careful notes.

Maybe it was dog language.

I was hoping, of course, to look professional and experienced in front of Leopold Zimmer. But with Dagwood in my group, I figured my chances weren't great. The surprise was that it wasn't Dagwood who caused the problem. It was Swampwater. She lay down and wouldn't move. I had to drag her over to the leashing area. Then, as soon as her leash was on, she glued herself to Brutus.

Doggy love! This was getting *really* silly. Not to mention embarrassing in front of Leopold Zimmer. Swampwater smartened up when we got outside, trotting along in a straight line and even leading the pack. But she still managed to stay on the edge of her group, right next to Brutus, who stayed on the edge of *his* group.

Okay, I could live with that.

I was eager to start quizzing Leopold Zimmer about dog language, but – rats! – Gaylene was talking so much that poor Leopold couldn't get a word in sideways. On and on she went, all about the dog books she'd read, the animal behaviour she'd observed, the courses she'd taken in animal psychology and … wasn't she *ever* going to stop?

Leopold Zimmer smiled and nodded and smiled and nodded, but finally he started to wear out. Telling Gaylene he had a particular interest in cocker spaniels, he moved over to my group.

"The spaniel's name is Sally, you say? What can you tell me about her, Stevie?"

"You mean, about her secret language? That's what you're researching, isn't it? The secret language of dogs? Well, Mr. Zimmer – Leo – I don't really speak dog. I mean, I can *almost* understand cat, because I've owned a cat forever. His name is Radical, and he has plenty to say, believe me. But I was kind of hoping that *you* could maybe teach me a little dog."

"Teach you dog?" Leopold Zimmer laughed. "I'm afraid it's not that simple, Stevie. It's not like French or Spanish, you know."

"Yeah, well, okay." Obviously, I wasn't explaining very well. "But what if a dog had something really important to communicate? Like if she had … I don't know … witnessed a crime or something. Could you get the facts?"

"Hmmm." Leopold Zimmer scratched his head. "That's an interesting problem. I might not get the complete message, but I could probably get an idea. Do you have a particular situation in mind?"

I nodded. "And it's urgent. I mean, the information inside this dog is … well, important. In fact, a couple of lives depend on this information. Kids' lives."

"Their lives?" said Leopold Zimmer, alarmed.

"Oh, the kids aren't going to die or anything," I said quickly. "It's just that without this information, their lives are going to be ruined. Totally. Hopelessly. Forever. They might as *well* be dead."

"I see," said Leopold Zimmer, with a slow nod. "Well, Stevie, I'd be glad to try to help. Why don't we –"

But that was just about as long as Gaylene could stay out of the conversation.

"Leo?" she called. "Oh, Leo? Have you noticed what Daphne is doing with her teeth? Would you consider it a sign of frustrated aggression? Or is it simply normally assertive canine behaviour?"

Rats, rats, rats! Just when Leo and I were getting somewhere. Just when my miracle was about to happen. If I'd had an apple, I would have cheerfully stuffed it, whole, into Gaylene's mouth.

I tried to get Leopold Zimmer's attention back, but it was no use. Anyone who could top-dog Brutus could certainly top-person me. Gaylene top-personed Leopold too. Every time his mouth opened, she cut him off. After a while he gave up and just listened.

It wasn't until we were on our way back to Barking Buddies that I remembered Dinny.

"Gaylene!" I cried, interrupting her in the middle of a sentence – it was the only way. "I forgot to tell you. Dinny phoned. She's coming over in –" I looked at my watch "– half an hour. She said 'Hi' to you, too, Leo. She's looking forward to seeing you again."

"Dinny? Terrific!" Leopold Zimmer beamed. "But did you say half an hour? What a shame. I have an appointment at the university in half an hour."

"You do?" Gaylene and I both said it at the same time in the same way. A disappointed moan.

"But, Leo," said Gaylene, her face drooping, "I was planning on ordering in some lunch. There's a place down the street that has wonderful cheese croissants."

"Sounds great," said Leopold Zimmer, "but I really do have to run. Possibly, though ..."

"Yes?" said Gaylene and I together. She shot me a filthy look.

"Well, I might be able to come back tomorrow. Would that work?"

"Certainly," said Gaylene at the same time that I asked "Couldn't you come back this afternoon?" I was thinking about Deke Rifkin. Who knew when he'd show up again? Maybe I didn't *have* until tomorrow.

Leopold winked at me as he headed for his car. "I'll do my best."

I spent the next half hour cursing myself. One lousy chance at a miracle, and I let it get away. Maybe if I'd jumped Gaylene, held her down, tied her to a tree with the dog leashes …

Nah. I wasn't strong enough.

Anyway, I was too nice. It's one of my problems in life.

Anyway, Leopold Zimmer would probably have untied her.

Rats!

At eleven thirty, Dinny limped in, doing this funny little hopping thing with her left leg – the one with the grapefruit knee. She was wearing black stretch pants, so I couldn't actually see the knee, but I could see the bulge. Even so, Dinny looked cheerful, with a red bandanna around her neck and a big, pink-lipstick smile.

"Gaylene! Stevie! It is soooooo good to get out. I am sick to death of being cooped up in the house." She glanced around. "Where's Leopold?"

"An appointment at the university," said Gaylene, a sour note in her voice.

"Oh." Dinny was obviously disappointed. "I was looking forward to talking to him. Well, next time ..."

"How's the knee?" asked Gaylene.

"I'm getting around, as you can see. But it will be a long time before I ride my bike along the Sea Wall again, that's for sure."

I froze.

"What?" I croaked.

The Sea Wall is a path along the ocean. It runs around the edge of Stanley Park – where the president's dog was stolen!

CHAPTER 15

DINNY SMILED. "MY KNEE, STEVIE. IT'S PUT MY NEW exercise program on hold for a while."

"Exercise program?" I repeated.

"Cycling."

I probably looked a lot like a fish at that point – eyes popped, mouth open. At any rate, Dinny laughed.

"You look like you've just been hit over the head," she said.

In a way, I had.

"Uh, Dinny?"

"Yes?"

"When was the last time you rode your bike? On the Sea Wall, I mean?"

Dinny frowned. "Sunday morning. That's how I hurt my leg. Stevie, are you all right? You look pale."

"My mom said you hurt your knee taking out the garbage."

"Well, that's what finished me off – tumbling down the back steps of my house." Dinny hop-walked over to the desk to leaf through her mail. "But the reason I fell was – I had already twisted my ankle earlier, in Stanley Park."

I don't know what I looked like on the outside, but inside, I was a mess. A big fight had just started in my brain. One part was saying "No way! Dinny is one of your mom's best friends. She's never pulled a prank in her life." Another part – the detective part – was screaming "Stanley Park? Sunday morning? And the dog ended up in *her* day care? Are you listening, Stevie Diamond? Are you putting this together?"

Dinny and Gaylene went back to the playground to talk about Brutus. I stayed in the office, chewing my fingernails off, one by one. Usually fingernail-biting helps me straighten out my thoughts, but not this time. There was a battle going on inside me, and all the fingernails in the world weren't going to stop it.

Dinny? The Prankster?

Nooooo …

Yes?

Nooooo …

When Jesse walked in, I was so glad to see him that I almost hugged him.

I said almost.

"Any sign of Rifkin?" he asked, looking around.

I shook my head.

"Good. It's your lunchtime, right? Want to go to that pizza joint up the street?" He peered at me. "Something wrong, Stevie? You look kind of white."

"Pizza," I mumbled. "Sure. I'll pay."

"You'll pay? Boy, something's *really* wrong. What's going on?"

It wasn't till we were sitting in a booth in Pass-Me-Da-Pizza, slices of Mediterranean Special in our hands, that I told him. He was almost as amazed as me.

"Dinny? Your mom's friend? No!"

"Yes," I said.

"No!"

Talking to Jesse was as bad as talking to myself.

"Listen, Jesse, all I'm saying is we'd better add her to our suspect list."

You don't know how much I hated to say that. Dinny comes to all my birthday parties. Sometimes she even makes the cake. Angel food with lemon-coconut icing. Her specialty.

The suspect list weighed a ton as I took it out of my pocket.

"So," I said as I slowly added Dinny's name, "now we're up to four suspects."

Jesse shook his head. "Nope."

"What do you mean, nope?"

"I mean, I got a hold of Matthew today. Austin's friend. He was at a chess camp over on the east side of town, but I tracked him down." Jesse grinned proudly.

"And?"

"Cross Austin off your list, Stevie. He's not the Prankster."

The news sent a piece of green pepper down the wrong way in my throat. After a bit of coughing and a couple slurps of water, I managed to ask, "How do you know?"

"Well, me and Matthew, we talked for quite a while. About all kinds of things – guy things, you wouldn't be interested. Anyway, I finally worked the conversation around to last Sunday. Just to see if Matthew knew where Austin was that day."

"And?"

"They were together, Stevie. *Out of town* for the whole weekend – in Victoria. Seems there was some big computer show on, with hot new programs and games. You know these guys – they had to see it."

I thought hard. "Are you sure Matthew's not lying?"

Jesse shoved a large piece of pizza crust into his mouth. "I'm sure. We were in the same drama class last term. That guy is the worst actor on the planet. No way could he fake this story."

"But what about all those clues?" I asked. "The article Austin was reading about the president's dog? The way he was staring at Swampwater?"

Jesse reached for a fresh piece of pizza. "Well, that's the other thing. After I talked to Matthew, I went to see Austin. You know, over at the math camp? Gee, Stevie, you wouldn't believe how badly I did in that placement test. After all that work I did last term on square roots, I end up –"

"Jesse?"

"Yeah?"

"Austin?"

"Oh, right. Could you pass me the Parmesan cheese, please? Thanks. Well, I managed to get Austin on his own, and, well, I found out why he's been doing all that stuff. The spying and all."

"How?"

"How what?"

"How did you find out?"

"I asked him."

"You *asked* him?"

Jesse nodded and took another bite.

"You just came right out and *asked* him why he's been reading articles about the president's dog? You *asked* him why he's so interested in Swampwater?"

Jesse grinned. "Yup!"

I groaned. "Haven't you ever heard the word 'secret,' Jesse? How about 'confidential'? Can't you –" Oh, what was the use? "What did Austin say?"

Jesse giggled. A piece of mushroom flew out of his mouth and landed on the tablecloth. "Well, that's the funny part. You know how we've been suspecting Austin of stealing the president's dog? Well, guess what? He's been suspecting *us* of the same thing. He saw that picture of Marietta and the president, and *he's* been detecting *us.*"

Hooting away, shoving in more pizza, Jesse didn't even notice that only one of us was laughing.

"You mean," I said slowly, "Austin Alderson *knows* that Swampwater is Marietta? He *knows* we've got the president's dog?"

Jesse let out a burp. "Well, I guess he does now. I mean, now that we've talked about it and everything. But he's been suspicious all week."

There are times when I wish that my business cards didn't say "Diamond & Kulniki, Detective Agency." There are times when I wish they just said "Stevie Diamond, Detective."

This was one of those times.

I couldn't believe it. Jesse practically confessed! To one of our suspects, yet.

"Listen carefully," I said. "Did you tell Austin what really happened? How we *found* the dog? How we didn't steal it?"

"Of course," said Jesse. "What do you think I am?

Stupid? I told him the whole story."

"And?"

"And what?"

I sighed. "Did he believe you?"

For the first time, Jesse looked uncertain. "I'm not sure. Well, maybe ... I don't know."

"What, exactly, did he say?"

Jesse picked up a paper napkin and started tearing it into strips. "He said ... um, let me see ... yeah, he said he was glad I'd told him and that I should be glad, too, because I'd gotten it, um, off my chest."

I couldn't speak. Not a word. Just stared at the top of Jesse's head. The waitress put the bill on the table.

Jesse finished tearing the napkin to bits, glanced at me, peered out the window, and then gulped loudly. Finally, he was starting to get it.

"Uh, Stevie? You don't think old Austin's going to, like, turn us in ... to the police. Do you?"

I didn't answer.

"Nah," said Jesse. "Not old Austin. Not ... oooooh, mommy!" He clapped both hands over his face.

"It probably doesn't matter," I said. "*Somebody's* going to turn us in, that's for sure. What difference does it make whether it's Deke Rifkin or Austin Alderson? Either way, we're left holding the Prankster's bag."

"But – but –" Jesse's eyes darted around desperately. "Can't we give the police our suspect list?"

"Sure we can. But first, we'd better add our *own* names. In giant letters. Right at the top. Because if we don't, the police will."

Jesse put one hand on his forehead and pushed

the pizza away with the other. "Want this, Stevie? I'm not hungry any more."

I shook my head. "I'd better get back to Barking Buddies. And Jesse? Keep your fingers crossed. We have only one hope left."

Jesse blinked. "What's that?"

"Leopold Zimmer. He said he might come back to Barking Buddies. If he does, I'm going to get him together with Swampwater. Those two are going to communicate if I have to lock them in the bathroom together and hold the door shut with my teeth."

"Yeah," said Jesse, nodding hard, "and if you need ... er, more teeth, well, you know who to call."

"Thanks." I stood up.

"Uh, Stevie?"

"Yeah?"

"The bill?"

I paid on the way out. I didn't mind, even though Jesse had eaten most of the pizza. After all, I was earning big bucks at Barking Buddies. But even that thought made me gloomy. There probably wasn't much chance to spend your money in jail.

Hurrying back to work, I had all my fingers crossed that Leopold Zimmer might have returned. He hadn't. Dinny was gone, too – another piece of bad luck. I was hoping to question her some more. On the bright side, there were no police cars surrounding the dog day care.

Gaylene had three of the dogs already leashed up, ready for me to take out – Dagwood, Sally and Bonbon. I added Swampwater and stalled as long as I could, hoping Leopold might turn up. Eventually

Dagwood started climbing the shampoo racks, so I had to leave.

When I returned an hour later, still no Leopold. Yeah, I know. He didn't say he'd come for sure. But I can't help getting my hopes up. It's like a disease with me. Tell me "maybe" and I'll hear "yes" every time.

All afternoon I felt jumpy. Whenever I heard a car outside Barking Buddies, I got this awful bad feeling and this terrific good feeling, both at the same time. The bad feeling was fear – was it Deke Rifkin and a car jammed full of police officers? The good feeling was excitement – maybe it was Leopold Zimmer, here to communicate with Swampwater and save me and Jesse from a life of crime and desperation.

In the end, nobody came. No Rifkin and no Leo. Only the dog owners when they came to pick up their dogs.

Austin Alderson's eyes were as big as fried eggs when he walked in. He stood in the front doorway for at least a minute, watching every move I made. Twitchy as a mouse's whiskers, he didn't even hear Gaylene until she'd spoken to him three times.

"I *said* – could you ask your parents to phone, please? We really need to discuss Brutus's behaviour. Austin? Are you listening?"

"Yeah. Sure. Brutus. Behaviour."

I fetched Brutus from the playground. When I handed the leash to Austin, he got so rattled he dropped it.

Gee. You'd think I was on the FBI's most wanted list.

Wait a minute. Maybe I *was* on the FBI's most wanted list!

That thought followed me all the way home.

Dinner that night was one of my favourites – ravioli in tomato sauce with garlic bread – but I could hardly get it down. Sitting there between my parents, I had a terrible urge to confess, to spill every last detail of the horrible mess. My parents would believe me. They'd know the whole thing was just one silly accident and coincidence after another. They'd know that Jesse and I weren't the Prankster … wouldn't they?

Sure they would. But who would believe *them?* Still, I'd feel a lot better just getting it off my chest … wouldn't I?

As I shoved the raviolis in slow, goopy circles around my plate, I realized that my dad was talking to me.

"… so pleased you got this job, Stevie. Besides the money, which you can put towards clothes or college, there's the valuable job experience. It'll help a lot when you look for part-time work later, in high school."

"Absolutely," said my mom. "I mean, it's awful that Dinny hurt her leg. But what an opportunity for Stevie!"

Speaking of Dinny …

"Listen, Mom. Remember how you told me that Dinny wrecked her knee taking out the garbage?"

She nodded. "Aren't you going to have any garlic bread, Stevie? I made an extra-large loaf, mostly for you."

"Sure. But, Mom, Dinny came in to Barking Buddies today. She told me she hurt her leg at Stanley Park."

My mom speared a ravioli, chewed and swallowed. "Right. Stanley Park *first,* when we were riding our bikes. But that was just a twisted ankle. It didn't even stop Dinny from riding. It wasn't until she got home and went to take out the garbage – you know how steep her back stairs are – that her ankle gave way and she fell on her knee. I guess the ankle was weakened from twisting it in the park."

Was I hearing right?

"Wait a minute," I said. "Did you say 'we'? 'We' were riding our bikes in the park?"

My mom plucked a cherry tomato from her salad, tossed it into her mouth, and looked up, surprised. "Sure. Me and Dinny and Gaylene. We went for a ride early Sunday morning. It was going to be just me and Dinny, but Dinny invited Gaylene along. I gather she doesn't have a lot of friends. Anyway, we rode all around the park. Then we had brunch at the English Bay Café and rode home together. It was great! You were still asleep when I got back – around noon." She looked confused. "I told you all this, didn't I?"

"No … you … didn't."

"Oh." She shrugged. "Oh well. No big deal. Stevie, is there something *wrong* with your ravioli? Come to think of it, you haven't eaten much the last couple of nights. Are you on some weird diet or something?"

"Gotta go."

"Go?" My mom dropped her fork with a clatter. "Go where? Stevie! You haven't finished your dinner!"

"Jesse's house! Save it for me, Mom." I hoped she heard me. I was charging through the door as I yelled it.

Jesse came to the door munching on a veggie-burger. "Hi, Stevie. You hungry? My mom left me a whole –"

"Never mind that." Rushing inside, I slammed the door behind me. "Our suspects are disappearing faster than rabbits in a magic show, Jesse. We've lost two more!"

"What?"

"We have to cross Dinny and Gaylene off our suspect list. They have a perfect alibi."

Jesse snorted. "Perfect?"

"My mom!" I groaned. "She was with them – both of them – all Sunday morning. Unless you think my *mother* is the Prankster, we have to cross Dinny and Gaylene off the list."

"But, Stevie," he stammered. "That means –"

"I know." I collapsed onto the white loveseat. Usually I worry about the furniture in Jesse's house – a single fingerprint would show up – but tonight I was like a drowning girl hurling herself onto a raft.

"It means," I said, "that we have exactly *one* suspect left." I pulled the suspect list out of my back pocket and stared at it. "Baby Lawrence's mom."

"But," said Jesse nervously, "we don't even know who she is."

"Right," I said.

"Or where she is."

I nodded.

"In fact," said Jesse, "we don't even know if there really *is* a Baby Lawrence."

"Exactly."

"And we haven't seen Baby Lawrence's mom since Tuesday morning."

"Precisely."

"Oh, Stevie, this is bad."

"Jesse," I said, "you have no idea. And *don't* start calling for your mommy. It's not going to help."

Jesse relaxed his lips, which had already started to form an "m." He began taking jerky little steps instead, kind of bouncing on his toes.

"Stevie?" he said after a minute. Bounce, bounce.

"Yeah?"

"What are we going to do?"

"Jesse, how come you always ask *me* that?"

He did a couple more bounces, stopped and shrugged. "Because you always know?"

Oh. Well, that was nice ... I guess. It took me a moment to realize that he was right. I do know. Maybe not always. But at that moment, in that living room, in that house, yes. I knew.

"We're going to think," I said.

"Think?" said Jesse. I could tell he was hoping for something more exciting.

"It's all we've got left. Our brains. We are going to sit here, all night if we have to –"

"Oh, gee, Stevie, I'm not sure my mom will let –"

"All night," I repeated firmly, "and we are going to go over every single detail. We are going to think until our brains hurt. We are going to think until our skulls quiver. We are going to think and think and think, Jesse, until we figure out some angle on the Prankster!"

Jesse's mouth opened. His eyes glowed.

"Think," he repeated softly. "Yes. It's simple. Straightforward. I like it. You figure it'll work?"

I shrugged. "Got any better ideas?"

He shook his head. "Let's get started."

CHAPTER

JESSE FOUND A THICK PAD OF YELLOW PAPER, WHILE I sharpened a bunch of pencils in his mom's electric pencil sharpener. Then he made a big pot of wild berry tea and set it in the middle of the kitchen table, along with a plate of ginger-snaps.

"We'll start at the beginning," I said, reaching for a cookie, "and go through this whole week. There's got to be *something* we've missed."

So that's what we did. We thought and remembered and wrote things down and talked and ate cookies and drank tea and thought some more. When Jesse's mom came home from work at ten o'clock, we were on our second pot of tea and halfway through the yellow pad.

"What's up?" she asked, peeking into the kitchen.

"Project," said Jesse.

His mom, of course, could only think of school projects. "On your spring break?"

"Best time," said Jesse, dunking a cookie. "Your brain's fresh."

His mom smiled. "I'm off to bed. Don't stay up too late."

Seeing Mrs. Kulniki reminded me to check in with *my* parents.

"What about your four-footed friends?" asked my dad. "Swampwater ate Radical's dinner, and now Radical's crouched on top of the fridge. I think he's planning an ambush."

"Could you feed Radical please, Dad? And put Swampwater in my room? I'll probably be late. This project we're working on ... it's sort of ... overdue."

By midnight, Jesse and I had come to the end of our memories. They were all there, in that stack of yellow pages.

"So what have we got?" Jesse plunked a bowl of popcorn on the table.

"I'm not sure," I said, skimming through the scrawled handwriting.

We'd managed to remember, and write down, a lot of little things that had happened since Sunday. The problem was, they didn't add up to much. The yellow pages were filled with odd bits and pieces – things like the nasty way Brutus had gone after Mrs. Worthington's dog, Pugsley. And the colour of Baby Lawrence's carriage – blue. And the research notes in Leopold Zimmer's notebook – that I didn't get a chance to read. Even Deke Rifkin's broken nose got in there.

It was like a jumble sale. Tons of junk. Still, somewhere in every jumble sale, there's got to be a treasure or two.

"Why don't we focus on Baby Lawrence's mom?" said Jesse. "After all, she's the only real suspect we have left. Did you spot her on any of your other walks? Maybe *without* the baby carriage?"

I thought for a moment, then shook my head. "What about you? Did you notice anything odd or unusual about her?"

Jesse shrugged. "She was a mom. Who looks? The only thing *I* noticed that morning was Swampwater's yipping. I thought my eardrums would explode. Hey, Stevie, maybe that's a clue. The yipping."

I shook my head again. "Swampwater yips all the time."

We sat there for another hour, sifting through those yellow pages like archaeologists uncovering an ancient city. Bit by bit. Carefully. Going over and over the same ground. Every now and then, I'd get the barest hint of some kind of connection. A wisp. A glimmer. But when I tried to grab on, it always disappeared.

"Can't stay awake, Stevie," said Jesse at ten after one. He was slumped over the table, eyelids drooping, chin resting on his arm. "Not one more minute."

"Jesse, no. We can't quit. Drink some tea."

"No more tea. I'll drown." His words were slurred. "Gotta get some sleep."

"You can sleep tomorrow."

Too late. His eyes were closed. His cheek twitched. A trickle of drool dribbled down his chin.

"Jesse?" I shook his arm, but that just made his head wobble back and forth. "For crying out loud, we don't have *time* to sleep."

Time. It had become our worst enemy. Now that it was Friday, Deke Rifkin would have to act. This was his last chance to get the dog back before the president left on Saturday morning. And then there was Austin Alderson. The guy was a walking time bomb. Any second, he could grab a phone, dial the police, and turn in two of his best friends in the whole world.

Well, okay, maybe not *best* friends. But we *did* go to the same school. It should count for something.

It's over, I told myself, walking home through the dark courtyard. Jesse and I had done our best – my brain felt like a squeezed orange – but it wasn't good enough. Might as well get some sleep. Tomorrow we'd have to Face the Music. That's what Ms. Rizzolo calls it when someone in class gets caught doing something wrong and is about to get punished. Facing the Music.

The pets were both asleep. I muttered a quick "Thanks" to my dad. Radical was snoring in his bunk – or maybe he was purring. Sometimes I can't tell the difference. Swampwater let out a soft whimper from his cardboard-box bed, and then a whine. A doggy dream, I guessed.

Do you think dreams are catchy? You know – like giggles or yawns? If so, maybe it was Swampwater's doggy dream that got me going that night. Or maybe it was all that brain activity, or the tea sloshing around, or even the steady hum of the clock beside my bed. All I know is, I had hardly closed my eyes when I had one of the wildest dreams of my life.

It started with me walking across the Burrard Street Bridge – that's a long arched bridge that leads towards Stanley Park. I was just strolling along, feeling pretty good, until I began to realize … slowly, the way it happens in dreams … that someone was *chasing* me.

I started to run. Hey, even in dreams, I'm not dumb.

I ran as hard as I could, but whatever-it-was kept coming. I glanced back.

Oh noooooo …

My suspects! All of them! Red-faced with fury, they raced behind me at top speed – Gaylene, Dinny, Austin and Baby Lawrence's mom.

Gaylene, in the lead, wore a white karate outfit and slashed at the air with vicious karate chops. Beside her ran Dinny, in a pair of shorts. She had – ugh! – no knees. Just a coconut in the middle of one leg and a pineapple in the middle of the other. Her long fingers reached out like bananas to grab me.

Aaaaagghh … run, Stevie!

Austin Alderson was charging along beside them, dressed in a blue police uniform. Waving a nightstick and blowing a whistle, he yelled over and over again, "Stop! In the name of the law!"

Run!

Behind Austin, but catching up fast, ran a woman in a track suit. It was Baby Lawrence's mom, and she was hurtling along like an Olympic sprinter, pushing an enormous baby carriage that bounced up and down like a basketball. But what was this? A baby sat up in the carriage and started shaking his fist at me. Baby Lawrence? No, it was Deke Rifkin. Then another baby head popped up – Leopold Zimmer! And another – Mrs. Worthington! The babies lurched back and forth as the carriage bounced, shaking their little fists and yipping at me.

Yipping?

Yes, yipping. Oh, this was too much. They were *all* yipping now – the whole dumb gang that was chasing me. The noise was deafening.

"YIP! YIP! YIP! YIP! YIP!"

Putting on a fresh burst of speed, I charged towards the top of the bridge. The yipping faded. Exhausted, I was just starting to slow when I heard a new sound, even scarier.

Growling.

Terrified, I looked over my shoulder.

Aw, no ... pleeeeeese.

A pack of wild dogs! Slathering, howling. I saw with a jolt of shock that one of them was – Daphne! And there was Walter. Lulu. Napoleon. Shep. Dagwood. Sally. Brutus. But they were so much *bigger!* So much *meaner!* Their teeth had grown. Their claws had sharpened. Their eyes gleamed yellow. Brutus was in the lead, foaming at the mouth, his fangs the size of carving knives, and he was gaining on me. Aaaggh! Brutus! Iiiiiyy! He was right behind me! Snarling! Snapping! Growling! Flangs slashing! Spit flying! He was going to leap! They were all going to –

I sat up in bed.

Panting.

Sweating.

My heart was pounding so hard, I don't know how it stayed in my chest. Around me, the covers were tangled and snarled, scattered all over the bed.

Man ... what a nightmare.

I shuddered.

I sat there like that for maybe ten minutes. Finally, finally, my body started to calm down. My heart slowed. My breathing eased off. Closing my eyes, I tried to go back to sleep.

Hopeless.

I was way too shaky.

So I lay there with my eyes wide open. Thinking. Just like I'd been thinking all evening. Like a clock that couldn't stop ticking, my mind ran over the details again – all the clues, all the things that had happened. I could see those scribbled yellow pages in my mind as clearly as if they had been in front of me. There *had* to be a pattern to the Prankster's crimes. That's what the police always looked for – a pattern. If only I could *see* it.

I must have laid awake for an hour. Finally, I started to drift. My mind relaxed. A gentle purr from the bunk beneath me soothed me back towards sleep.

And then – with a suddenness that made my breath stop – I saw it. The pattern!

How had I missed it before? It was as plain as the freckles on my face. Stevie, I thought, you're an idiot, you're a fool.

But never mind that.

I saw the pattern. I got it now.

I *knew* who the Prankster was.

CHAPTER 17

"INCREDIBLE!" SAID JESSE, BLINKING HARD. "STEVIE, THAT'S really hard to believe." Finally, after twenty minutes of talking, my words were starting to penetrate his grogginess.

"Believe it," I said. "It's the only thing that makes sense."

He scratched his head. "You're right about the handwriting. And I believe you about the yipping. But still … it's so weird."

Jesse's mom hadn't been happy to see me at their door at eight in the morning. It had taken some fast talking to convince her to wake up Jesse. Throwing in the word "emergency" two or three times had helped.

Now we were outside, under the huge maple tree at the back of the courtyard. Jesse's checkered shirt was buttoned wrong. One side hung longer over his jeans than the other. His hair stood up in clumps, and he seemed to be having trouble focussing.

"Are you really awake?" I asked for the third time. "We have to make plans." I had slept late this morning – no surprise after last night. But I was due at Barking Buddies in twenty minutes, so I'd have to hurry.

Jesse rubbed his face hard with both hands. Then he blinked at me. "Ready for action, Stevie."

"All right," I said. "I *know* my idea is bizarre. But it fits, right? The trouble is – we need proof. That's where *you* come in."

"Me?" Jesse smiled crookedly as he tucked his shirt into his jeans. The collar still stuck up way higher on one side of his neck than the other. I decided to ignore it.

"You have to go to the library. It shouldn't be hard to find what we need. And if I'm wrong ..."

"We're sunk?" suggested Jesse.

I nodded. "Think Titanic."

Crossing his arms, he shivered. "What am I looking for?"

It took me another minute to explain. The whole time I was talking, I was wondering – was Jesse awake enough to take this in? His eyes were still glassy and had that fake-open look, as if invisible fingers were holding the lids apart.

"Got it," he said a couple of times in a flat robot-like voice.

"Jesse, are you sure? I have to go now."

Yawning, he nodded. "Got it."

"Okay. I'll meet you outside Granville Market at ten thirty. We'll plan our next move there."

Here's how I had it figured. When the library opened at ten, Jesse would – I hoped – be the first one in the door. Ten minutes for him to find the information. Then he could hop on his bike and race over to Granville Market, which was on my main dog-walking route. I would make sure I went dog-walking *alone* this morning, and I'd work it so the dogs and I were outside Granville Market at exactly ten thirty.

Simple, right?

I arrived on time at Barking Buddies. No police cars parked outside. Good.

With Gaylene, I was a regular sunflower – smiling cheerfully, offering to help. I was so cheerful, in fact, that she gave me a few strange looks – especially when I admired her earrings, which, to tell you the truth, weren't all that exciting. Gold hoopy things. But mostly she was pleasant, too. Probably because it was my last day. She agreed right away when I said I'd like to do a "solo walk."

"Kind of like – you know – graduation," I said.

"Oh, I understand," said Gaylene quickly. "Off you go."

After leashing up Swampwater, Daphne, Sally, and Dagwood, I headed for the door. But there was a problem. Swampwater wouldn't leave Brutus. When I tried to pull her away, she had a pretty good trick – she just sat down beside him. Have you ever tried to pull a sitting dog?

Gaylene pursed her lips.

"How about if I take Brutus?" I offered. Walking Brutus again made me nervous, especially after his escape with Swampwater. But sticking around Barking Buddies made me even *more* nervous. Any second now, Gaylene was going to say we'd have to go walking together.

Letting Dagwood go, I leashed up Brutus. Brutus and Swampwater were thrilled and showed it by scampering and play-wrestling.

"Save it," I muttered. "Let's get out of here."

Outside, I felt better. The dogs had a lot of energy and charged along like a team of sled dogs, but I still had more than an hour before I had to meet Jesse. Plenty of time to wear them out.

Wear *me* out, too. As I walked the last few blocks to the market, I was breathing hard.

Granville Market is this huge wooden structure right beside the ocean, full of fruit and vegetable stands, meat counters, chocolate sellers, doughnut shops, fish and chip joints ... well, you can get almost anything you want to eat in there. That's one of the reasons I'd suggested it as a meeting place. I'd missed breakfast and was hoping Jesse would run in and get me a snack. Something that would help my brain work better.

French fries, for instance.

As I rounded the last corner, I was already excited. Jesse should be waiting right outside, clutching the proof. Finally, we could get ourselves out of this mess. Finally, we could –

What on earth?!

There was a crowd outside the market. Crowds are normal *inside* the market – it's a popular tourist place – but this was weird. For a second, I got scared. Had something happened to Jesse? I looked around for ambulances.

What I saw was worse.

Limousines. Police motorcycles.

Uh-oh.

I forced myself to ask.

"Excuse me," I said to a short blonde woman. "What's going on here?"

"The market's closed, dear." She backed away from Brutus. "The summit leaders are visiting inside."

Oh, great. Perfect. Why now? Those guys had all *week* to tour Granville Market. Did they have to pick the exact moment that Jesse and I were meeting there? This was twice in three days that they'd gotten in our way. Were they following us or what?

Okay. Better not get too close. In fact, better get far away.

But what if I missed Jesse? He could be in the middle of that crowd, looking for me.

I led the dogs to a spot at the edge of the crowd near a large green garbage dumpster. Usually it held mashed cardboard boxes. Today it was locked. Most people wouldn't even have noticed it, but I *happen* to be an expert on dumpsters, having ended up inside one in a previous investigation. I knew, for instance, that there'd be footholds on the outside that I could stand on to get a good view. I got a solid grip on the leash knot with my right hand and used my left to hoist myself up.

Perfect. My perch made me at least two heads taller than everyone else. I searched the crowd for Jesse's straight brown hair – probably still not combed. I saw grey hair, black hair, hats, blonde hair, bald heads, red hair, caps. Lots of brown hair too, but not the hair I was looking for.

"Jess-seee!" I called, but only a few people close to me heard and turned their heads.

"JESS-SEEE!"

A white-haired man in front of me put his hands

over his ears.

Hopeless. Also risky. We were way too close to the president. I hopped down from the dumpster. Jesse would just have to find me on my way back, or turn up at Barking Buddies. We could talk later, at lunchtime.

Uh-oh. Problem. The crowd had shifted, and now it surrounded the dumpster. Did you ever try to walk four dogs through a crowd? Some people reached out to pat them, but others edged away in alarm. Some people did *not* like to be dog-sniffed, even in a friendly way, and especially not by Brutus. There were oohs and eeks and little squeals as we tunnelled our way through. Then Brutus started to growl, and that made people even *more* nervous.

Oh boy. Better get out of here – fast. I looked around for an open space.

Yes. There!

"Come on, guys," I said to the dogs. "This way."

I pulled them through the crowd towards the open space. Some idiot had his arm out straight, blocking the way. I shoved, but he wouldn't move it, so I ducked under. The dogs followed.

Good. We were in the open.

Not good.

The idiot was a police officer.

He was one of a long *line* of police officers. They all had their arms out straight, holding back the crowd. They were staring at me and the dogs with expressions of shock and horror.

Nothing like *my* shock and horror. The dogs and I were right in the middle of a path the police had cleared from the market to the limousines – a path for the summit leaders!

And there they were. I could see their suits as they stepped through the market doors.

Worse – Swampwater could see them! She went absolutely bananas. I have never seen anything – human, animal, fish, bird or reptile – go into such a frenzy. The barking! The leaping! The pulling! The jerking! Even the police were amazed. Too amazed to move for a couple of seconds, and by then it was too late.

Don't get me wrong. I held on to the leash knot. Even in all this hysteria, I knew it would be a disaster beyond my worst dreams to let a giant German shepherd charge into that group of suits. I held on to that leash knot as if my life depended on it.

But one leash slipped loose.

Swampwater.

The escape artist.

She ran at lightning speed towards the group of suits. There were yells and gasps. Police officers leaped at her like football players pouncing on a football, but she was too fast.

The last thing I saw, before huge, heavy hands gripped me above the elbows, was a flash of yellowish brown dog leaping through the air at the silver-haired president.

CHAPTER

WITHIN FIVE SECONDS, THERE WERE MORE BADGES around me than fleas on an alley cat.

It wasn't easy, but I finally convinced them to take me back to Barking Buddies. The police, I mean. After loading the three remaining dogs into a police van, they stuck me in the back of a police car. They wanted to take me "downtown," but I managed to convince them there was important evidence back at Barking Buddies.

"Listen, uh, Stevie," said the cop in the passenger seat. "I think it would be a good idea for you to call your parents."

I took the car phone she offered and started dialing.

Maybe *some* parents wouldn't mind being phoned at work by their daughter, who happens to be sitting in the back seat of a police car. My parents weren't that cool.

"What?" squealed my mom. "How? Who? When? I'll be right there. Where?"

My dad wasn't quite as bad. He made a few choking noises, but once he got his voice back, he was almost sensible.

"Stay right where you are," he ordered. "I'm on my way."

Stay. Sure thing. As if I could do anything else. A large-sized uniform got into the car on my left, and an extremely large-sized uniform got in on my right. A police sandwich – and guess who was the filling?

"Aren't I supposed to … uh … call my lawyer or something?" I asked, as the car started moving.

Nobody answered.

I tried again.

"I've seen that on TV. You know … about calling your lawyer."

Silence. The big guys beside me stared straight ahead.

"Doesn't matter," I mumbled. "I don't even *have* a lawyer."

I wish I could have taken a picture of Gaylene's face as I walked into Barking Buddies with half the Vancouver police force crowding in behind me. She was talking to Deke Rifkin, but as more and more blue uniforms filed in, she started gulping instead. Her skin went the colour of wet cement. Outside there were even more police officers – I could see them through the window. I could also see TV trucks and crews, and a small crowd gathering to see what all the excitement was about.

Then I spotted my dad, struggling through the TV people before getting stopped by the police. He was gesturing and pointing and showing identification. My mom, meanwhile, had made it to the door, a uniformed police officer at her side.

"There she is. That's my daughter. Stevie, is it true? That funny-looking little dog belongs to the president of the United States?" Looking a little shaky, she dropped into a plastic chair.

Before I could answer, my dad burst in.

"Stevie! Valerie! What's going on?"

Both my parents started talking at once. Gaylene got her voice back and chimed in, too. Meanwhile, I was keeping a lookout for Jesse. Where was he anyway? More importantly, how was he going to get in? If my parents had had trouble, what chance did *he* have?

"Stevie?" It was a grey-haired man in a rumpled suit. He had one of those droopy, pouchy-cheeked faces with big bags under the eyes – kind of like a bloodhound. "My name is Detective Halliday. I'd like to ask you a few questions."

"Shoot," I said, then winced. Bad choice of words. Halliday didn't seem to notice.

"Suppose you start by explaining how you got that little yellow dog. The one that ran away at Granville Market."

My dad nodded anxiously. A police officer started taking notes.

Okay. No choice.

Face the Music, Stevie.

I told them the truth. First, how we had found Swampwater in Barking Buddies on Sunday. I described what a mess she'd been and – this was hard – explained how Jesse and I had turned her into a *worse* mess. A green, shaggy, half-bald mess.

"Henna?" said my mom. "*My* henna? Stevie, didn't you read the package?"

"Mom, there wasn't time. I – oh, never mind." I told them how Jesse had spotted the newspaper article about Marietta and how we had figured out that Swampwater was the president's dog.

"It seems to me," said Halliday quietly, "that *that* would have been the perfect time to turn the dog over to the police."

"I know," I said, swallowing hard. "But don't you see? People would have thought that *we* were the Prankster. Jesse and me. We have juvenile minds, right? Just like the Prankster. We're medium height and athletic. Jesse has a black mountain bike and – and a whole shoebox full of Prankster articles."

The note-taking officer started writing faster. Oh geez, what was I doing? Talking them into arresting us? Even my mom and dad looked suspicious.

"But we aren't – uh, didn't!" I said, scrambling for words. "We couldn't! We –"

"Now, why don't we just slow down a little," suggested Halliday. Leaning back in his chair, he crossed his legs and twiddled his fingers, like he had all the time in the world.

Yeah. Slow down. Good idea.

"Jesse and I *didn't* steal the dog," I said, pausing to let it sink in. "But we know who did."

Halliday's thick body jerked up straight. "You do?"

I had everyone else's attention, too. I could feel it in the way they all leaned towards me. I could hear it in the sudden silence in the room.

Into that silence came a shuffling sound from the direction of Pooch Playground. It was followed by a familiar voice. "Stevie?"

Jesse's upper arm was in the grip of a police officer who had to be close to seven feet tall. Where did they *get* these guys?

"I found this kid crawling over the back fence," said the giant.

"I had to," whimpered Jesse. "They wouldn't let me come in the front way."

That's when I noticed what was under his left arm – the one the police officer wasn't holding.

"Is that it?" I asked, hardly daring to breathe.

He nodded. "You were right, Stevie. Look!"

Breaking loose from the giant, he ran over and handed me the book. I flipped open the back cover and grinned.

"I assume," said Halliday with a cough, "that our fence climber here is this friend you've been talking about. Jesse? Excellent. Now then, you were saying … you have information about the identity of the Prankster?"

I nodded. "Jesse and I have been working on it all week. At first, we were totally on the wrong track. We thought maybe Austin Alderson – he's a kid from our school – was the Prankster. Or Gaylene Schultz there." I pointed.

Gaylene's face went pink, then red, then white, then red again. "Bu– wha–" she said.

"It's okay, Gaylene," I said. "We know it's not you."

I turned to Halliday. "You see, it wasn't till last night that we finally started thinking about all the *other* people we've run into over the last week. And it wasn't until last night that Jesse mentioned the yipping."

"Yipping?" repeated Halliday.

"It's this horrible sound that Swampwater – uh, Marietta makes," I said. "Sounds like someone's stepping on her tail. I realized last night that it was a special yip. You see, Swampwater doesn't yip *all* the time. She only yips at certain people."

"And who might they be?" asked Halliday, crossing his arms.

I glanced at the note-taking police officer. "Be sure to get this down. It's important."

He rolled his eyes. Hmmph. He'd be sorry.

"First there was this guy in a brown leather jacket. He had weird orange hair – the colour of carrots. We ran into him on the street on Monday, the first morning I went dog-walking. I didn't know who he was, but Swamp– Marietta yipped at him.

"Then," I added, "late that same night, when I was asleep, Marietta started yipping again. She woke up the neighbours. At the time, I didn't realize it, but she was yipping *at* someone – someone who was out in the courtyard beside my house, slashing the tire on my bike."

"I heard Swampwater yipping that night," offered Jesse. "I also heard her the next morning, when she yipped at Baby Lawrence's mom. Man, what a racket."

"Excuse me?" said Halliday, confused. "Baby Lawrence's mom?"

We were losing him. Quickly, I described the woman with the baby carriage who had pasted me to the sidewalk on Tuesday morning.

"Baby Lawrence's mom," Detective Halliday repeated. Shaking his head, he sighed heavily. "I hope there's a point to all this."

"There is," I promised. "The next person Marietta yipped at was Mrs. Worthington. That was on Wednesday."

"Mrs. Worthington?" piped up Gaylene, eyebrows raised. "That distinguished older lady with the Pekinese?"

I nodded. "At the time, all I noticed was Brutus going after Mrs. Worthington's dog, Pugsley. But now I realize – it was Marietta who *started* the fight by yipping at Mrs. Worthington."

"Exactly what I said at the time." Gaylene was triumphant. "Swampwater started the trouble."

"Are we coming to the end here?" interrupted Halliday.

"Almost," I told him. "The last time Marietta yipped was yesterday. She yipped at Leopold Zimmer, the famous dog author."

"That's right." Gaylene nodded. "She *did* yip at Leo. She got Brutus so worked up, he jumped on the poor man. It was the oddest thing. Somehow I expected all the dogs to love Leo."

"Leopold Zimmer," repeated Halliday dryly. "Okay? That's it for the yipping?"

I nodded and glanced over at the police note-taker. "Maybe you could read that back."

The officer looked startled, but I guess he couldn't figure out how to say no. "Carrot-haired man in leather jacket," he read out loud. "Person in courtyard at night. Baby Lawrence's mom. Mrs. Worthington. Leopold Zimmer."

"Hmmph," said Halliday, with a frown that cut deep wrinkles into his forehead. "I'm not saying this hasn't been fun, but … what are you saying? That one of these people is the Prankster?"

"No," I said.

"Excuse me?"

"Not one of them. *All* of them. They're *all* the Prankster."

You could actually hear it – the sound of dozens of breaths being sucked in. Then there was a rapid babble of conversation. The note-taker was scribbling like mad.

"Five Pranksters?" said Halliday.

"No," I replied as the room became silent again. "Not five Pranksters. One Prankster – in five disguises."

"Actually," said Jesse, "it's six."

"Six?" repeated Halliday.

I nodded. "When the Prankster showed up at Barking Buddies in his *sixth* disguise, Marietta didn't yip at him, but that was only because she had escaped and wasn't even here at the time. The Prankster's sixth disguise is as ..."

I pointed across the room. "A Secret Service agent. And there he is! The *fake* Secret Service agent, Deke Rifkin!"

CHAPTER

FOR A SECOND, EVERYONE LOOKED AROUND, BAFFLED. Snake that he was, Rifkin had slunk behind one of the giant cops, hoping to escape notice. But when the cop saw where I was pointing, he stepped aside.

"The Prankster!" said Jesse.

Rifkin had made himself as small as he possibly could – not easy with those wide shoulders and that barrel chest. I couldn't see his eyes behind his dark glasses, but his head swivelled back and forth like he was searching for an exit.

With all those police in the room, he didn't have a chance, and he knew it. Around him, officers were muttering, trying to figure out how Rifkin had even gotten in there.

"Who is this guy?"

"Do you know him?"

"No, do you?"

"Wait a minute," interrupted Halliday, holding up a hand. He pointed at Rifkin. "You, sir, stay where you are." Then, turning to me and Jesse, "Listen, kids. With the first five people you mentioned –

okay. You say that Marietta was so scared of the man who stole her that she made a frightened yipping sound whenever she saw him?"

"Right," I said. "All those disguises didn't fool Marietta. Dogs recognize people by smell. Marietta knew it was the Prankster every time. She tried to tell us by yipping. But we didn't understand."

Halliday scratched his head. "Well, fine, but how does *this* guy figure in?" He pointed a thumb at Rifkin. "You said Marietta *didn't* yip at him, right?"

I nodded. "Jesse and I identified Rifkin through a different clue. His handwriting."

Jesse took over. "I saw the Prankster's handwriting in Stanley Park – on the sidewalk where he wrote that note. I told Stevie afterwards that it looked just like Ms. Rizzolo's. She's our teacher. The Prankster's writing looked just like a teacher's – all neat and perfect."

"Last night," I said, "when Jesse and I were thinking about the case, we remembered Deke Rifkin's handwriting. It was neat and perfect, too."

"It looked *exactly* like the Prankster's," said Jesse. "But it wasn't till Stevie mentioned it this morning that I made the connection."

"Leopold Zimmer *also* had that neat teacher-type handwriting," I added. "I saw it yesterday in his notebook."

Gaylene looked stricken. "Leopold Zimmer. I can't believe that one of the world's most respected dog authors is involved in a shabby business like this."

"He's not," I said.

"But you just said –"

"The Leopold Zimmer we met yesterday wasn't the *real* Leopold Zimmer, Gaylene. It was the Prankster pretending to be Leopold Zimmer. The real Leopold Zimmer looks like this." I held up the book Jesse had brought from the library. It was a hardcover copy of *Everything You Ever Wanted to Know About Dogs*. Unlike the paperback copy that I had been reading, this one had a photograph of the author inside the back cover. The man in the picture was about sixty years old, round as a pillow, and almost totally bald.

"*That's* Leopold Zimmer?" said Gaylene, squinting at the book. "Why, he's a little old dumpling."

I nodded. "The Leopold Zimmer *we* met was a total fake."

Halliday turned to Rifkin. "Okay, buddy, your turn. What do you have to say about all this?"

For a moment, it looked like Rifkin was going to deny everything. He puffed out his shoulders, clenched his jaw, and gave Halliday a top-dog stare – just like you'd expect a Secret Service man to do. He looked as if he might try to bluff it out.

But the top-dog stare that Halliday gave him back was the real thing. Rifkin sagged.

"It's over, Deke," muttered Jesse. "Time to face the music."

Slowly, Rifkin stepped forward. He took off his sunglasses. Then he removed his suit jacket so we could see the football pads that had bulked out his shoulders and chest. Next he reached up and pulled off the brown wig. The moustache came next – a little bushy strip. Finally, his nose.

Well, not *all* of it. Just most of it. The nose he was

left with was a medium-sized regular sort of nose.

The man who stood there was no one I had ever seen before. I mean, I'd seen *parts* of him. I recognized Mrs. Worthington's chin and Leopold Zimmer's ears and Baby Lawrence's mom's nose. But the guy himself? A stranger. A perfectly ordinary stranger. Medium thin. Ordinary height. Average looks. Someone you would never notice in a crowd.

"My name," he said, "is Bob Jones. I am the man you know as the Prankster."

CHAPTER

FOR ABOUT TEN SECONDS, NOBODY MOVED. THEN Jesse asked the question that was on everyone's lips.

"Why?" He stared, dumbfounded, at Bob Jones. I could tell he was thinking about his shoebox full of articles. "Why'd you do it? Pull all those weird pranks?"

Bob Jones sank onto a plastic chair and ran his fingers through his thin greying hair.

"I'm not sure that any of you will be able to understand," he said. "You see, I'm a writer. I don't write about dogs – the girl's correct about that. No, I write novels. I've been writing them for ten years. Recently, I finished my fifth."

"Hmmm," said my dad. "Bob Jones? I don't believe I've read –"

"Of course not." Bob Jones's mouth dropped into a pout. "*Nobody* has read *any* of my novels. They're all in a closet in my bedroom. I send them out to publishers, but nobody wants to publish them."

"Why not?" asked Jesse.

"Because they're boring. Every one of them.

Boring, boring, boring! And do you know why?"

Nobody answered.

"Because I'm boring! My life is boring. Even my name is boring. Bob Jones! What kind of name is that for a writer? Look at me. I'm a walking yawn."

"Wait a minute," I said. "I thought people wrote books out of their imaginations."

"They do," sighed Bob Jones. "That's my other problem. No imagination. Do you know what colour my socks are? Grey! All of them. Do you know what I have for lunch? A cheese sandwich. Every single day of my life. See what I mean?"

He stared glumly at the floor. But when he raised his head a moment later, a sparkle came into his eye. "Six months ago, I had my first really good idea. What if I found a way to *make* my life more exciting? What if I found a way to get close to some really exciting people? Wouldn't it rub off? Just a little?"

"The Prankster?" said Jesse.

Bob Jones smiled as if he'd eaten something delicious. "Yes, the Prankster! Oh, it's been such fun. I've met such fascinating people. That Chicago Bull, for instance – we had a wonderful conversation through the broom-closet door. A little one-sided, of course, but I enjoyed every awful, angry word he said.

"And the disguises!" he went on, rubbing his hands together. "They've been the most fun of all. I was disguised as a stagehand when I snatched the opera singer's toupee. I was a maid when I snuck into the prime minister's hotel room. At the basketball game, I was wearing a grizzly bear costume. Do you know, you can go almost *anywhere* at a sporting event when you're dressed as the team mascot? And lately – well, just think. I've been a young mother, a Secret Service agent, a wealthy doctor's wife and a famous dog psychologist. All in one week!"

Halliday stepped closer and cleared his throat. "Mr. Jones, before you go any further, it's my duty to tell you that you have the right to retain counsel."

I knew what that meant – Bob Jones could call a lawyer. Halliday said some other stuff about Bob Jones's rights and how he'd have to write his story down in an official police statement.

"I'm going to have to ask you to come along now," said Halliday. "We'll take your statement at the station."

"The station?" Bob Jones looked heartbroken at the thought of giving up his audience. Then he noticed the reporters pressed up against the window and the TV cameras peering in.

"Just a moment." Whipping out a comb, he ran it through his thinning hair. He cleaned his teeth with his tongue and straightened the front of his shirt.

"Anyone got a mirror?" he asked.

When nobody answered, he held out his arms for the police. "I'm ready."

As the door opened, the photographers' lights flashed and the video cameras started to whirr. Bob Jones stepped into the crowd with his police escort – and an enormous smile on his face.

❖ ❖ ❖

He made a full confession at the police station. Jesse and I managed to get a peek at it in Halliday's office after we wrote *our* statements. Jesse kept saying we shouldn't look. He said the statement was police property, and it was probably against the law to peek, and if we weren't careful, we'd end up sharing the Prankster's cell. But *I* said that if Detective Halliday didn't want us to see the statement, he wouldn't have left it on the edge of his desk when he stepped out.

Anyway, here they are – Bob Jones's exact words:

Written Statement of Robert Jones

The first time I saw the dog – on TV, the night the president arrived – I knew I had to have her. What a kick it would be to own the president's dog! Even if I couldn't tell anyone who she really was, she would still be the ultimate addition to my Prankster collection.

Now, I don't know a lot about dogs, but I do know they have to be walked. The president's hotel was right beside Stanley Park, so I had a pretty good idea of *where* the dog would be walked.

I "borrowed" my neighbour's mountain bike – he'd never miss it – and got myself a biking outfit and a mask. After that, it was just a matter of waiting. I was hoping the president would walk the dog himself, but I guess that was too much to ask. Anyway, when his secretary came out with Marietta on Sunday morning, I was ready. I followed them into the park.

My chance came at the water fountain. The secretary stopped to take a drink. Stealing the dog was so easy, it was almost embarrassing. I just raced up, snatched the leash, grabbed the dog, and rode hard.

How could the secretary possibly catch up on foot?

She couldn't, of course, and I was laughing to myself as I slipped away. But I didn't laugh long. The dog got hysterical. She drove me nuts with all that yipping. I stuffed her into a basket on the back of the bike and raced out of the park and across the bridge.

That's when I lost her. Just as I got off the bridge, she wiggled out of the basket and ran down beside the water. There's some wild brush there, and she disappeared into it. I looked and looked, getting filthy with burrs and mud, but I couldn't find her anywhere. I can't tell you how mad I was. When it got dark, I went home.

In the morning, I went out to look for her. I searched underneath the bridge and on all the streets nearby. On one of those streets, I saw a couple of people walking a bunch of dogs. Well, that caught my interest. I looked closer. One of the dogs was green. I was getting a little chuckle out of that when the green dog let out a yip. Imagine my shock. It was Marietta!

I had no idea how she'd ended up green, of course, but it looked like getting her back would be simple. I put on a leather jacket and a red wig that I keep in my backpack for emergencies, and I walked right up to the dog-walkers. What I didn't count on was the German shepherd. That is one big animal. Mean too, and keen to protect Marietta. As soon as I got close to her, he started growling and snapping. Between that and Marietta's yipping, well, I figured I'd better back off.

There had to be another way.

I followed them back to that dog day-care place and hung around, hoping to catch Marietta *without* the German shepherd. Marietta did come out eventually, but this time she was in the kid's backpack. The kid got onto a bike and rode away.

Stealing a dog out of a backpack that's on a kid who's on a moving bike – well, that looked tricky. So I followed the kid home. Later that night, I snuck into the courtyard outside her house and slashed her bike tire. I figured that if she was on foot, it would be a lot easier to grab the dog.

Next morning, I disguised myself as a mom, snitched a baby carriage out of a backyard, and found a good spot to ambush the kid. My plan was simple: grab the dog, ditch the carriage, and run away. Unfortunately, the kid brought another kid along – that boy. He got in the way of everything, and the dog took off, yipping like mad. Man, was I cheesed.

I decided that the only thing to do was get inside the dog day care. For that, I'd need a dog. I borrowed my Aunt Flora's dog, a rotten little Pekinese named Pugsley. Pugsley the Pain, I call him. I snuck a few of Aunt Flora's clothes, too, and worked up a pretty good imitation of the old doll. Then, calling myself Mrs. Worthington, I strolled into Barking Buddies, hoping to grab the dog. But I never got the chance. The second Marietta saw me, she started yipping again. And that got the German shepherd going. They ganged up on me. It wasn't fair. I had to leave.

That was Wednesday morning. By Wednesday

afternoon, I was feeling desperate. I figured that if I showed up disguised as a Secret Service agent, they'd *have* to give the dog to me, whether it yipped or not. So Deke Rifkin was born, and I went to Barking Buddies again – this time to *demand* the dog. Unfortunately, Marietta had run away. That was a real blow.

I thought she was gone forever.

Still, I kept my eye on the kids as they left Barking Buddies. And darned if Stevie didn't come out carrying Marietta in her arms. Was she *lying* about losing the dog? I couldn't figure it out.

I decided to make one more try to get inside. This time I had a terrific idea. When I'd shown up as Mrs. Worthington, I'd heard Stevie and Gaylene talking on the phone to some famous dog expert. He said he was coming to do research next week. Neither of them had ever met him and that gave me my next brainwave. Why couldn't *I* be Leopold Zimmer? Fake teeth, a wig and a false nose should do it as a disguise. And if I skimmed Zimmer's book, I could fake it as an expert. I'd tell them I needed to study the little green dog more closely and – presto! – Marietta would be mine.

It didn't work out that way. The problem was Gaylene. It was like she was glued to me. Frankly, I don't see how the real Leopold Zimmer is ever going to get any research done at Barking Buddies if Gaylene treats *him* that way. The other problem was the owner. She made a sudden decision to come in that day. When I heard that, I had to beat it. Dinny knows the real Zimmer. I wouldn't have fooled her for a second.

All week, as I've tried over and over to grab the dog, it's been one frustration after another. If only I'd managed to catch the kid and the dog alone and on foot – even once – I'm *sure* I could have gotten Marietta back. But no. One day they're on a bike. The next day, the kid's mom comes to get her. Another day, it's her dad. The boy was hanging around all the time, too. And that big dog – Brutus! I'm telling you, the kid was as heavily guarded as the Mona Lisa.

Today was my last chance. I decided to give the Deke Rifkin disguise another shot. So I show up at Barking Buddies, and I wait around half the morning. And what does the kid do? She walks in with the entire Vancouver police department and then points the finger at *me.*

I'm telling you, it's almost funny. A kid! All that stuff I pulled and got away with … half the cops and reporters in Vancouver on my trail, and me laughing at them … and in the end, who figures it out?

A kid.

Makes you wonder, doesn't it?

Signed,

Bob Jones

(alias the Prankster)

CHAPTER

IT TOOK ABOUT A WEEK FOR THINGS TO SETTLE DOWN. We got interviewed by a bunch of reporters, but we never did get on TV. We didn't get our pictures in the paper, either. I guess the reporters thought Marietta was cuter, even with her funny haircut. There were pictures of *her* everywhere. The captions underneath said dumb things like "The Dog Came Back!" and "Marietta Makes a Home Run." There were a lot of pictures of Bob Jones too. He was grinning at the cameras in every one – even the ones that showed him being led into the police station in handcuffs. You think he'd be embarrassed.

He wasn't. Not even when the police searched his house and found his collection of stolen property. The opera singer's toupee. A baby carriage – that had never had any Baby Lawrence in it, ever. A mountain bike belonging to Bob Jones's neighbour. A purple hat and a white coat belonging to Bob Jones's Aunt Flora. A silver toothbrush belonging to Mick Jagger. A set of fondue forks belonging to the mayor of Vancouver. And, of course, the prime minister's underwear.

The only place we did get our pictures in was our school newspaper, *The Beacon*. Unfortunately, the photo was a little blurry. In fact, it was hard to tell which face was mine and which was Jesse's. That's because Evangeline Patterson-Blakely, who took the picture, always jiggles the camera.

The real thrill was the letters. Both Jesse and I got letters from the president, thanking us for looking after Marietta. Thanking us! He didn't even mention the haircut and dye job. It just goes to show, doesn't it? If you love someone (or something), you don't really care what they look like. You'd think if you were president of the United States, you'd be embarrassed by a crummy-looking dog like Swampwater. But, no, the president held Swampwater up proudly for the cameras. I was impressed. I was impressed by the letter too, which was on *extremely* fancy paper. The signature was real. You could tell by turning the paper over and seeing the dents from the president's pen.

We also got letters on fancy paper from the prime minister of Canada and the mayor of Vancouver. The prime minister thanked us for recovering his luggage. He didn't say a word about underwear, but you wouldn't really expect him to. And our letters from the mayor – well, they were a complete surprise. We didn't even *know* about the fondue forks.

Anyway, Jesse and I were in a pretty good mood when we biked down to Granville Market the following weekend. I figured I was still owed those fries I had missed on my last visit. So we were heading for the fish and chip place when Jesse spotted a magazine at the news-stand.

"Stevie, look! It's Marietta!"

There she was on the cover – in colour. Almost all the green was gone from her coat, and even the yellow wasn't so bad. Jesse quickly handed over the money for a copy.

"I bet our picture's in here, Stevie. Gee, I've never been in a magazine before."

We found a place to sit down, and Jesse flipped through the magazine, looking for the article.

"Look!" he said. "Here's Swampwater and the president. And here's a picture of the prime minister – and a big picture of Bob Jones. And … gee, Stevie, I don't see us anywhere."

"Read the story, Jesse. We've got to be in there somewhere."

I waited while he glanced through.

"WHAT!!" The word came out like an explosion. Jesse smacked the pages together in disgust.

"What's the matter?" I asked, rescuing the scrunched magazine.

He snorted. "They called me *Jeffrey* Kulniki!"

I skimmed the article. It took awhile because neither of our names showed up until the third page. Finally, there they were – Jeffrey Kulniki and – WHAT!! – *Steve* Diamond. The next line said we were "two local *boys* who had provided the police with helpful information."

"Jesse, look. It says I'm a boy! It says my name is Steve."

Jesse gawked at the page. "That's sick."

"You bet it is." I turned the page, looking for more. "I can't believe this. It hardly mentions us. It's all about Bob Jones and Marietta and the president."

Jesse nodded, disgusted. "Did you see this?" He pointed. "It says Bob Jones is writing a book. He's going to call it *Marietta and Me*."

"Marietta and *him?*" Now I was really teed off. "He hardly got near Marietta. *We* had her for a whole week."

"You bet we had her! All those baths? My skin is still wrinkled." He held out a hand as evidence.

"Marietta and him!" I snapped back. "Ha!"

"Ha!" agreed Jesse. "I can't believe it. Jeffrey."

We sat there, fuming, as we searched the article one last time.

"It's not fair," said Jesse. "First we don't get on TV, and now this!"

"Outrageous," I muttered.

But then, catching sight of Jesse's red scowling face, I couldn't help it. I giggled.

"What are you laughing at?" The scowl deepened.

I laughed harder. "Jesse, do you remember why Bob Jones got into all this trouble in the first place? Remember his police profile?"

"Sure. Athletic, juvenile –" He stopped. Grinned. "Oh. It's the 'looking for attention' part, right?"

"Right," I said.

Jesse's smile turned a little sheepish. "So you're laughing because we're looking for attention, too?"

I nodded, thinking of Gaylene and all the strange things *she* did because she didn't feel sure about herself. "I guess my dad's right. Everybody wants to be noticed. Everybody wants to feel special. The trick is not to get weird about it."

Jesse grunted. "I just want them to get my name right. Jeffrey. Geez."

"Forget it. Let's get something to eat."

"I can't," said Jesse. "I spent all my money on this stupid magazine." He jammed it into his back pocket.

I was still feeling rich from my week at Barking Buddies. "I'll buy."

Ten minutes later, we were sitting on a bench by the wharf outside the market, eating fish and chips (me) and chocolate-sprinkled doughnuts (Jesse). The sunlight glinted off the ocean and seagulls flew, squawking, around us, hoping for a hand-out. A little kid in a red wool hat was chasing pigeons, making them take off in a noisy flutter of grey and white wings, not even noticing when they came down again right behind him.

"Do you remember being a little kid and chasing pigeons?" I asked, dropping a hot, vinegary, salty french fry into my mouth.

"Of course," said Jesse.

French fries. Sunshine. Pigeons.

No dogs.

It was just about perfect.

"Stevie?"

"Uh-huh?"

"You know what's funny? Bob Jones kept saying he had no imagination. But look at all those disguises he came up with. He had *tons* of imagination."

"You're right." I let my eyes droop shut. Sunlight danced on my lids, making yellow-red swirls of colour. "Maybe he just had trouble *using* his imagination. Adults are like that sometimes. Haven't you noticed?"

"Uh-huh," said Jesse. "Not us kids, though."

I shook my head. "No way."

We sat in silence.

"When I was a little kid," said Jesse after a while, "I used to imagine there was this gigantic tiger living under my bed. I was afraid he would grab me by the ankles, so I used to leap all the way from the door to my bed in one jump."

"Jesse?"

"Yeah?"

"How would a gigantic tiger *fit* under your bed?"

"I don't know. He just did."

I smiled. "When I was a little kid, I used to imagine that all big rocks had money inside them. Gold coins. I thought that all you had to do was break a rock open, and you'd have enough money for the rest of your life."

"Stevie?"

"Yeah?"

"Did you ever try it? You know ... break a rock open?"

"All the time."

"Did they ever break?"

"Nope."

"So maybe it's true," said Jesse. "Maybe there *are* gold coins inside."

I smiled again. "Maybe."

For the next few minutes, we just sat there listening to the gurgles of the pigeons and the cries of the gulls.

"I bet we could write a great book," said Jesse finally. "You and me."

I sat up straight and grinned. "Like about a president's dog that gets stolen and a couple of kids who dye it green?"

Jesse shook his head. "Nah. Something way more exciting than that."

"Okay," I said. "But not right now, okay?"

"No," he said, "we're way too busy right now."

We leaned back against the bench and closed our eyes.

"Any doughnuts left?" I asked.

"Sure." He passed the bag, and I took one out.

"Thanks, Jeffrey."

He laughed. "No problem, Steve."

ABOUT THE AUTHOR

Linda Bailey lives with her family in Vancouver, British Columbia. Like Stevie, she once caught a glimpse of an American president, who had come to Canada for a summit meeting. A few weeks later, she spotted a dogwalker walking eight dogs. The two incidents came together to give her the idea for this book.

Other books in the Stevie Diamond Mystery series:

What's a serious detective like me doing in such a silly movie?

How can a brilliant detective shine in the dark?

How can a frozen detective stay hot on the trail?

Who's got Gertie? And how can we get her back!

How can I be a detective if I have to babysit?

How come the best clues are always in the garbage?